W9-BWZ-130

"Allie and Hannah are my daughters, aren't they, Morgan?" Tyler asked.

"No, Ty, they're my daughters." Tapping her chest for emphasis, Morgan went on, "They're Whittakers, end of story."

Folding his arms, he scowled down at her. Then his demeanor shifted, and he grimaced as if she'd sucker punched him. "Why didn't you tell me?" he asked in a quiet voice laced with regret.

"I didn't think you'd be interested," she shot back. "You walked out on me with no explanation, no forwarding address. I didn't think you were exactly father material."

Tyler absorbed that in silence, a woeful look settling into an expression she'd never seen on him before.

Gazing out the door toward the house, he turned back to her with the firm jaw she recalled so well. "I would've found a way to make it work for us. You know that. You never even gave me a chance."

Morgan had to acknowledge that he was right, and the twinge of guilt she felt grew more insistent even as she tried to reason it away...

Mia Ross loves great stories. She enjoys reading about fascinating people, long-ago times and exotic places. But only for a little while, because her reality is pretty sweet. Married to her college sweetheart, she's the proud mom of two amazing kids, whose schedules keep her hopping. Busy as she is, she can't imagine trading her life for anyone else's—and she has a pretty good imagination. You can visit her online at miaross.com.

Books by Mia Ross

Love Inspired

Mustang Ridge

Beneath Montana Skies

Liberty Creek

Mending the Widow's Heart
The Bachelor's Baby
His Two Little Blessings

Oaks Crossing

Her Small-Town Cowboy
Rescued by the Farmer
Hometown Holiday Reunion
Falling for the Single Mom

Barrett's Mill

Blue Ridge Reunion
Sugar Plum Season
Finding His Way Home
Loving the Country Boy

Visit the Author Profile page at Harlequin.com for more titles.

Beneath Montana Skies

Mia Ross

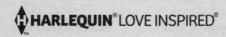

HARLEQUIN® LOVE INSPIRED®

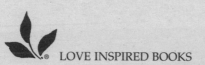

LOVE INSPIRED BOOKS

Recycling programs for this product may not exist in your area.

ISBN-13: 978-1-335-53895-6

Beneath Montana Skies

Copyright © 2018 by Andrea Chermak

www.Harlequin.com

Printed in U.S.A.

Forgive, and ye shall be forgiven.
—*Luke* 6:37

For all the people fighting to
keep our wild lands wild.

Acknowledgments

To Melissa Endlich and the dedicated staff at
Love Inspired. These very talented folks help me
make my books everything they can be.

More thanks to the gang at Seekerville
(www.seekerville.Blogspot.com), a great place
to hang out with readers—and writers.

I've been blessed with a wonderful network
of supportive, encouraging family and friends.
You inspire me every day!

Chapter One

"Hey there, cowgirl."

Holding a fifty-pound bag of sweet feed balanced on her shoulder, Morgan Whittaker froze in midstep. It couldn't be, she thought, before it occurred to her that was just wishful thinking. The once-familiar voice behind her could only belong to one person, and although she hadn't heard that smooth tenor in ages, she'd recognize it anywhere.

Very slowly, she turned halfway around and let her eyes confirm her suspicion. Thankfully, she was wearing her mirrored aviator sunglasses, so he couldn't see the contempt she knew must be plain in her eyes. "Tyler Wilkins. What're you doing here in Mustang Ridge?"

Under the brim of his cream-colored Stetson, the gold tinting his hazel eyes sparked with a bit of his infamous temper. But it quickly mellowed, replaced by one of those easygoing grins that had charmed her—and countless other women—for so long. "Well, now, last time I checked, this was my hometown, too. I haven't been to Montana in a while, so I figured it was time for me to make a visit."

"I'd say seven years is more than a while." For her, it was a lifetime ago. She was almost thirty now, and for her those days were a distant memory. From the look of things, nothing had changed for him, except that his rangy, athletic build had filled out a bit. He was more solid now, but she knew from hard-won experience that was just an illusion. There had never been anything solid about Ty. Unfortunately for her, she'd discovered the truth about him too late. "And since it's June, shouldn't you be headed to Reno for that big roundup I read about? The article said the humongous rodeo purse is drawing every able-bodied cowboy west of the Mississippi."

Something flashed across his weathered features, and for a brief moment she thought it almost looked like regret. Then again, the cocky bull rider had never been prone to remorse, even when he was clearly in the wrong. The look vanished quickly, and she decided it had just been a trick of the sunlight and shadows underneath the overhang that shaded the sidewalk in front of Big Sky Feed and Seed.

"Not goin' this year," he said simply, hooking his thumbs into his wide leather belt.

She noticed that he wasn't wearing his prized silver champions buckle because, really, you couldn't miss one of those if you tried. Something about him wasn't adding up for her, and while she shouldn't care, she had to admit that she was suddenly curious about what had brought him home. Figuring it couldn't hurt to ask, she dove in boots first. "Why not?"

He didn't answer, and when he took a step toward her, she instinctively pulled away. "What on earth do you think you're doing?"

"Taking that bag of feed before it caves your shoulder in."

Suddenly aware that she'd slumped a bit under the weight, she straightened up and glared back at him. "I'm perfectly capable of handling it myself."

"Suit yourself."

He didn't retreat, but he did drop his hands. Realizing that people were beginning to stare at them, she ignored his helpful gesture and heaved the bag into the back of her 4x4. She turned to catch him wearing an expression that struck her as being almost mournful before a half grin rushed in to replace it. "To answer your question about the rodeo, I'm just taking some time off. No big deal."

Any idiot could tell there was more to the story than that, but she didn't have the time or the patience to drag anything more out of him. Besides, he was obviously not keen to talk about it, or he would have spilled his guts to her already. She still couldn't believe he'd approached her in the middle of the street this way. Then again, he'd probably been hoping that a meeting in public would keep things between them more or less civil. Apparently, he'd gotten smarter since the last time she saw him.

She'd mostly recovered from the shock of seeing him, so she called up her backbone and opened the driver's door. "Well, enjoy your vacation. Bye."

She climbed into the cab and reached out to pull the door closed, but he stopped it with a strong hand scarred from years of rope burns and broken bones. Glancing down at the door and then up at her, he asked, "What's this decal for the Mustang Ridge Conservancy about? I've never heard of it."

"It's a new organization in town," she explained as patiently as she could. "There's a group of local residents working to make sure this area stays the way it is and out of the clutches of a big energy developer that's been sniffing around the last few months."

"Looking for what?"

"Natural gas and oil. That may or may not be under the ground, and may or may not be feasible to pump out of where it is."

A slow grin worked its way across the face that was still way too handsome for the good of any woman within ten miles. "You sound mad."

"I am," she spat. "What they've got in mind will destroy the environment, and the idea of it makes me furious. My family's been here on our original homestead for generations, and so have plenty of others. If we have anything to say about it, that land will stay the way it's always been."

"Sounds like a tough job."

"We'll figure it out." They had to, she added silently, because the alternative wasn't even worth thinking about.

"Speaking of your family, I was hoping to stop by and see JD while I'm in town. Ya think that'd be okay?"

Her father would probably take one look at his visitor and start choosing a shotgun from the rack in his den. In all honesty, Morgan thought that would be entertaining to watch. "It's fine with me. If he doesn't want to see you, I have no doubt he'll tell you so."

Ty stared at her through narrowed eyes, the brim of his hat adding an old gunslinger effect to the look. After a moment, though, that infernal grin was back in place. "We're neighbors, so we're gonna have to deal with each other at some point. No time like the present, right?"

Morgan didn't really care if he dropped off the face of the earth and was never seen again. But that sounded childish, even to her, so she went with a noncommittal shrug. "Whatever."

"My truck's over there," he commented, nodding to a flashy silver extended cab model parked across the street. It made her keenly aware that the mud-spattered vehicle she was driving was looking pretty ragged these days. "Mind if I follow you out there?"

"Whatever."

This time, he wisely let her close the door. She gave it a little more muscle than was strictly necessary, and the slam echoed off the two-story buildings that flanked both sides of the small Main Street business district. She started the engine, then noticed that he was still hanging in the open window, arms spread wide as if he was reluctant to let her go. Tamping down her impatience to be free of him, she glowered up at him. "Was there something else, Ty?"

"Yeah." After a deep breath, he grimaced and said the words she'd given up on ever hearing. "I'm sorry."

"For what?" she demanded, his remorse only adding fuel to her temper. "Slinking out of Houston in the middle of the night, or never having the guts to tell me why?"

"Both, and all the other things I did wrong with you. With us," he added in a somber tone. "You deserved better than what you got from me, but I want you to know that I honestly loved you."

A flood of long-buried emotions was threatening to swamp her good sense, but Morgan ruthlessly shoved them back into the dark recesses of her heart where they belonged. The boy she'd once loved had let her down in the worst conceivable way, and no matter how handsome or contrite the man standing in front of her seemed to be, she had no intention of letting him off the hook now. Or ever.

"Thanks. You know the way."

As she started the engine, he gave her the

kind of lost-puppy-dog look that she'd never seen from the arrogant cowboy she'd known most of her life.

"Can you forgive me?" he asked.

Angling a look at him from behind her sunglasses, she cocked her head in a show of considering his request. And then, because he totally deserved it, she brought the hammer down on him. "No."

With that, she shifted into Reverse and backed out of her spot, not caring whether she ran over his fancy riding boots or not. She caught sight of him in her rearview and tried not to be jealous of him as he strode across the street and beeped his truck open with one of those fancy new key fobs that did everything but order pizza for you.

Who did he think he was, anyway, she fumed while she sped out of town and toward the sanctuary of her family's ranch. Ambushing her like that, apologizing as if what he'd done to her was no big deal?

It had been an enormous, life-altering deal for her, and while things had turned out well enough, she resented the fact that he'd been able to blithely go on to enjoy a fabulous career when she'd had to sacrifice her own.

That was in the past now, she reminded herself, feeling the wind pick up as she increased her speed outside the town limits. Not far from the quaint shops and vintage theater, the scenery changed dramatically, and she felt her temper subsiding as she looked around her at the most beautiful place she'd ever seen. Mile after mile of wild beauty and rolling free-range pastureland flew past, broken up by ranches and small farms that seemed to be part of the landscape instead of built on top of it. Off in the distance the sun reflected off the southern face of the Bridger Mountains, giving them a cloud-like appearance that was still unlike anything she'd ever seen.

During her rodeo career, she'd traveled all over the country, racking up one barrel-racing trophy after another because she and her half-mustang palomino, Sadie, were just a tick crazier than their competition. But no city or town she'd ever been to could hold a candle to home. That was what made it home, she supposed as she turned into the long drive marked by a hand-carved sign that read Whittaker Ranch—1882.

Driving between long lines of board fence, she caught sight of her mare and smiled for the first time since Ty had rattled her in town. She pulled over and was mildly annoyed when he followed suit. Determined not to let him ruin her moment, she grabbed some dried apple slices from the stash she kept in the glove box and got out.

Sadie's ears perked up when Morgan came around the car and headed for the fence. Nickering a greeting, the gorgeous horse tossed her head like the diva she was and pushed against the top rail, craning her neck to reach the treats.

"Hold on to yourself," Morgan teased, using her father's equine version of hold your horses. Sadie angled a look at her, and she laughed as she held out a handful of Sadie's favorite snack. They were gone in an instant, and while she was snuffling around for more, she noticed Ty.

Blowing out an excited breath, she danced along the rail to where he was standing, arms spread over the top as if he'd been waiting for her to notice him. He showed her his empty hands, but apparently she didn't mind that he didn't have anything for her. Nosing under his palm, she nudged him into petting her cheek, then ruffling her forelock the way she liked.

"Traitor," Morgan grumbled, but the horse didn't seem to care that she wasn't happy.

"How are you, Sadie girl?" their unwelcome visitor cooed, a bright smile lighting his face. "It's been so long, I wasn't sure you'd remember me. Clyde's on his way, should be here day after tomorrow. Maybe we'll come by and you two can get reacquainted."

"If Clyde's coming, you must be planning to stay," Morgan said, hoping she sounded casual about the prospect. She'd assumed he was on vacation, and learning that he was planning to stick around awhile didn't exactly thrill her.

"Not sure right now," he hedged, rubbing Sadie's cheek in a pitifully obvious attempt to avoid Morgan's gaze.

Typical Ty, she thought bitterly. Look up *commitmentphobe* in the dictionary, you'd probably find his picture. Still, she couldn't shake the feeling that something was wrong. She didn't want to care, but there was a teeny tiny part of her that still did. Stupid, but true.

A bit of compassion for him bubbled free of her control, and she heard herself saying, "Well, I'm sure you'll get it all figured out."

Glancing up from under his hat, he gave her the kind of sheepish look she'd never seen on him before. "Thanks."

He'd stopped petting Sadie, and the spirited animal snorted her disapproval. Clearly out of patience, she gave another head toss before wheeling away from the fence and galloping off in the stunning burst of speed that had made her—and her fortunate rider—a champion many times over.

"Still gorgeous," Ty murmured, his gaze tracking the mare as she seemed to float over the ground. Then he looked over at Morgan, and his mouth crinkled in the boyish half grin that had first buckled her knees as a teenager. "Both of you."

It was a blatant attempt at getting on her good side, making her forget that he'd abandoned her after one of their infamous fights and had never looked back. Scowling at him for all she was worth, Morgan turned on her heel and stalked back to her car. That's what she got for showing him some sympathy, she railed silently as the engine roared to life and she jammed the transmission into gear. The sound of gravel spitting out from under the tires perfectly matched her mood as she flew up the driveway toward the house.

If Ty Wilkins thought a few sad looks and canned compliments were going to undo what he'd done to her, that cowboy had another think coming. Once he left town, everything would go back to the way it was before he showed up. She just wished he hadn't taken it into his head to make a detour to Mustang Ridge.

She could have happily lived the rest of her life never laying eyes on him again.

Still a spitfire.

The thought flew through Ty's mind almost as fast as Morgan's 4x4 was speeding away from him. During his long drive up from Texas, he'd spent a lot of his time picturing what it might be like when he encountered the fiery cowgirl again. Some of the scenarios had been downright frightening, to the point that he'd almost reconsidered the wisdom of his approach.

Then it had occurred to him that he owned nothing in this world except a few acres of land, some rodeo trophies and his truck.

Although the truck wouldn't be his much longer, he reminded himself grimly. He'd be delivering it to its new owner tomorrow, and then he'd start hunting for something he could afford. After hitting rock bottom a few months ago, he'd come dangerously close to being forced to sell his horse. By sheer, stubborn will, he'd managed to hold on to the prized cutting horse, but it had been a near thing. He'd gotten some insane offers, but even for a down-and-out cowboy, some things were priceless.

He might have lost everything else—in-

cluding his dignity—but he still had Clyde.
It was one of the few victories he could claim
recently. Actually, he amended as he eased
himself into the cab to follow Morgan, it was
the only victory. That was the unexpected
advantage he'd discovered in losing pretty
much everything you once considered important. Whatever you had left meant a lot
more to you.

At the end of the driveway was the same
sprawling farmhouse he recalled from his
childhood. Driving toward it, he admired
the menagerie of animals grazing in the two
pastures that flanked the gravel lane. While
they came across as gritty ranchers, in truth
the Whittakers were all softhearted critter
collectors who couldn't seem to turn away
anything that needed a home. Among the
kaleidoscopic herd of about twenty horses,
he spotted several goats, a cluster of sheep
and something that looked suspiciously like
a miniature camel.

The latter slowly raised its head, chewing
its cud in a back and forth motion that gave
its shaggy face a pensive appearance. When
it levered its head back and brayed, it made
Ty think of a tractor transmission grinding
to a halt in the middle of a field. That he still
remembered the death-knell sound from his

days as a farmhand was actually amusing, and he couldn't help chuckling. Some things stayed with you, he supposed, no matter how far away you've drifted from your roots.

Pulling into the circular turnaround near the house, he parked next to Morgan's car and winced as he slid to the ground. The back that had once been his strongest asset wasn't what it used to be, but bearing in mind what it had gone through, his doctors had told him that he was fortunate to be upright. Injuries like his weren't just career enders—they often turned out to be fatal. For some reason, he'd been spared that horrific fate, and whatever the future held for him, he was determined to meet it standing on his own two feet.

Like him, the Whittaker farmhouse had seen better days. Built of sturdy Montana pine, the framework looked as solid as ever, but the clapboards and roof were in need of some TLC. When the dog sprawled out near the front door caught sight of Ty, she jumped to her feet and trotted down to greet him much the way Sadie had.

"Hey there, Skye," he said, ignoring the protest in his back as he hunkered down to pet the speckled Aussie. "How've you been?"

She answered him with a short yip, turning her head to lick his palm in an obvious bid for more attention. When Morgan paused beside them, he looked up to find her staring down at him, arms folded in a gesture he couldn't quite read. When she didn't say anything, he figured it was up to him.

"It's nice to see some friendly faces," he commented, carefully unwinding to stand up. She didn't respond, and he decided to try some humor. "Even if they are furry and standing on four feet."

A hint of the wry grin he recalled teased the corner of her mouth, and when she removed her sunglasses, he saw a glimmer of appreciation in those incredible blue eyes. Her waterfall of blond hair was tamed back into a ponytail that fell down her back beneath her straw cowgirl hat, but a few of the curls he'd always admired had escaped to frame her tanned face in a cloud of gold.

On the day he met her in first grade, he'd believed Morgan Jo Whittaker was the prettiest thing he'd ever seen. In all the years he'd been on the rodeo tour, he'd met dozens of women, but he'd never come across one who even came close to changing that opinion.

Morgan was one of a kind, he thought for the millionth time. Beautiful, smart as a whip, with a sassy personality that both frustrated and fascinated him. And he'd walked away from her. What an idiot.

Now she was looking up at him, wearing a curious expression that made him feel like a bug squirming on a slide under a microscope. Trying to appear calm, he endured the scrutiny in silence, hoping it wouldn't last too much longer.

It didn't. "What are you really doing here, Ty?"

"I told you in town. It was time for a visit."

She took one step closer and stopped, those intelligent eyes boring into his with an intensity he'd rather not experience again. "You used to be a better liar."

That was true enough, and he couldn't keep back a chuckle. "Not enough reason to do it anymore, I guess. You want the truth?"

"It'd be a nice change of pace."

Stepping onto the porch, he motioned her to one of the handmade rocking chairs. When they were both seated, Skye plopped down on a braided rug between them, and for a single insane moment, Ty got a picture of how their life might have been if he hadn't messed everything up.

Behind them, a burly shadow appeared in the screen door, and Ty pushed himself to his feet. "Afternoon, JD."

With a "hmpf" that gave nothing away, the owner of Whittaker Ranch came through the door, letting it fall closed behind him with a sharp crack. His battered boots thumped ominously on the old floorboards, and Ty got the feeling of standing in front of an old-time sheriff, waiting for some kind of judgment on his character.

Sliding a quick glance at his daughter, JD leveled a cool glare at Ty. "I oughta run you offa this place at the end of a Smith & Wesson for what you did to my girl."

"I'm very sorry for everything that happened," Ty began, trying to keep his voice steady. He respected JD for many reasons, feared him for others. Right now, he was just trying to hold his ground and remember that he was nearly thirty years old and not the dumb kid he'd once been.

"Did you apologize to my Morgan?"

Ty loved the way he said it, as if she was a little girl still in need of her daddy's protection. Someday, if he was ever fortunate enough to have a family of his own, he'd be as fiercely protective of them as JD was of his.

"Yes, sir, I did." Looking over at her, he added, "I'm hoping she'll find a way to forgive me someday."

The lady in question didn't say anything,

but she wasn't glaring at him anymore, either. He took that as a positive sign.

Apparently, JD had noticed the same thing, because the old wrangler chortled. "I don't see any fresh holes in your hide, so you must've done all right. Are ya thirsty?"

"Parched. I left Denver around six this morning and didn't stop till I got here."

"Long drive." After a quick trip inside, JD came back with three glasses of lemonade. He handed them out, then settled onto the porch swing and crossed his boots on the porch floor in front of him. "So, what've you been up to?"

Ty nutshelled the past couple of years for his host, skimming over the worst of it to avoid a lot of questions he'd rather not answer just yet. Throughout the conversation, Morgan was unusually quiet, and he kept casually glancing her way to gauge her reaction to what he and JD were saying. Mostly, her face was maddeningly unreadable, and he found himself back in high school, wondering what was running through that quick mind of hers.

She'd always had a great poker face, and it seemed that she'd improved it over the years. Why she'd felt the need to do that, he couldn't imagine. While it wasn't any of his business, he couldn't help wondering what had caused her to cultivate such a close-to-the-vest attitude.

Suddenly, Skye bounced to her feet and darted off the porch to begin an easy herding lope up the long driveway toward the road. When a yellow school bus appeared in the distance, Ty chuckled. "Her hearing's better than mine. I never heard it till just now."

"I'm convinced that dog can tell time," JD announced confidently. "No matter what the school schedule is, she always seems to know when the girls are coming home."

"Girls?"

"My girls," Morgan explained, emphasizing the word *my* for some reason.

"I didn't know you were a mom, too. Is there anything around here you can't do?" Ty said, hoping to soothe her ruffled feathers with a little well-placed admiration. It wasn't all that hard, he mused. She was still the same remarkable woman she'd always been. There wasn't a day that went by when he didn't kick himself for leaving her behind.

"Not so far," she replied, arching an eyebrow in the haughty expression he recalled vividly. He'd been the target of that look far too many times to count, and it was burned into his memory forever.

The girls in question took their time walking up the driveway, with Skye flitting from one to the other in typical Aussie excitement. Ty got the impression that she was herding them toward the house, and he smiled at the picture. Country girls under a big, beautiful sky. Life didn't get much better than that.

As they drew closer to the house, he noticed something about them that made him stare over at their mother in surprise. "They're twins."

Morgan didn't respond, but JD proudly chimed in, "Allie and Hannah. Every bit their mama's girls, that's for sure. Hannah's sharp as a tack, and Allie's got a real way with critters, big and small. That's how we ended up with Teddy."

"Teddy?"

"The alpaca," JD clarified, nodding toward the odd animal Ty had noticed on his way in. "A friend of hers had to move away, and the family couldn't take livestock to their new neighborhood. Allie begged us to take him in, and—"

He ended with a shrug, and Ty laughed. "You couldn't tell her no. Why does that sound familiar?"

"Hey, now, that's not fair. He told me no plenty of times," Morgan protested.

"I was talking about your little sister, Jessie," Ty clarified, taking a drink of his lemonade to sell the comment to her. That got him the raised eyebrow again, and he couldn't keep back a grin. To his relief, the look mellowed slightly, and while she didn't exactly smile back, at least she wasn't glaring at him anymore.

When they saw who was sitting on the porch, the girls broke into a run, although one of them lagged behind by a few steps. As she got closer, Ty could see that she was doing her best to keep up with her faster twin but couldn't quite manage it. In response, Skye slowed her pace and circled around the girl, as if encouraging her to keep going. Something about that twanged his heart deep inside, in a way he'd never felt before.

Shoving away the baffling reaction to someone else's child, he waited for JD to make the introductions.

"Girls, this is Ty Wilkins, an old friend of ours who's back for a visit. Ty, this is Hannah—" he pulled one of them close "—and Allie." With her, JD paused a moment to let the comment sink in before smiling at her. After a couple of seconds, she answered with a faint smile before moving past him to where Morgan was sitting.

Ty didn't have much experience with kids, but he knew a shy girl when he saw one. Standing, he took off his hat the way he'd been taught and smiled at each of them in turn. "Ladies, it's a pleasure to meet you."

Hannah thrust a hand at him, shaking his with a firm confidence that reminded him of her bold mother. "Nice to meet you, sir."

Wow, that was a kick in the teeth, he mused. Made him sound ancient. Then again, to her he probably was. Allie didn't venture out to follow her sister's lead, and he settled for another smile in her direction. "Your grandpa's been telling me about how you ended up with an alpaca named Teddy. It was real generous of you to give him such a good home."

"He's a good boy," she allowed in a voice so quiet, he had to strain to hear it. After that, she patted Morgan's cheek and drifted into the house without another word.

Obviously, there was something different about her, but he'd never dream of asking what it might be. Fortunately, her twin filled in the blank for him. "Allie has a-tism, so she's shy around people. It was nice of you to talk about Teddy, 'cause she really likes him."

Following that very straightforward explanation, she skipped inside, Skye right on her heels.

The revelation hung in the air, creating an awkward silence that Ty had no clue how to fill. Morgan looked especially uncomfortable, and JD reached over to grasp her hand in a reassuring gesture. "Both our girls are special. That's what we focus on, right, honey?"

"Right." She made a valiant attempt at a smile that fell woefully short. Standing, she said, "If you'll excuse me, I'm going to check on things inside, then unload that feed I bought in town. Hope you enjoy your visit, Ty."

He suspected that she didn't come close to meaning that, but as she disappeared inside, he couldn't really blame her for not welcoming him with open arms. She'd told him she'd never forgive him, and he believed her.

"Well, I'd best get over to my place and see how bad that old cabin looks," he said, putting his hat back on before extending his hand to his neighbor. "Thanks for the talk and the lemonade. I enjoyed 'em both, just like always."

That leathery hand held on to his for an extra pump before letting go. Then JD gave him a sage look, as if he knew what Ty was keeping from them all. "You're welcome here anytime, son. Starting over ain't easy, but it might go better if you get a little help once in a while."

"What makes you think I'm starting over?"

"I was born during the day," the old rancher told him with a chuckle, "but not yesterday."

Grinning, Ty strolled out to his truck feeling a lot more chipper than he had just a couple of hours ago. As he drove out and headed for his place on the other side of the Whittakers' east pasture, something about Morgan's twins was nagging at him. He couldn't quite put his finger on it, but there was something about them that felt familiar to him.

They were both the spitting image of their mother, he reasoned. That must be it. But even as he tried out that explanation in his head, it didn't sit right with him. Then, because he couldn't think of anything else, he put it out of his mind. As JD had noted, starting over wouldn't be easy, but he had a lot of years left, and he had to come up with a productive way to spend them. What that might be, he couldn't say, because the only skills he'd ever had any interest in learning were useless outside the rodeo arena.

Beyond that, the modest Cape-Cod-style cabin he'd referred to hadn't been lived in since his parents had moved away five years ago. No doubt, there was enough work to do there to keep him well occupied and prevent him from thinking too much about the still amazing—and still maddening—Morgan Whittaker.

Chapter Two

"What on earth is Ty Wilkins doing here?" Morgan's little sister, Jessie, demanded in an outraged whisper.

"Visiting with Dad," Morgan replied evenly, keeping her voice down to avoid alerting her daughters that there was something amiss. She focused on the apple juice she was pouring, then reached into the cookie jar for some fresh molasses crinkles.

"And?"

Morgan ignored the question and set the snack on the scarred oak table that dominated the large country kitchen. "Girls, why don't you take your snack into Grandpa's den and watch TV? When you're done eating, take a whack at your homework. I've got some chores to finish up, but if you get stuck, I'll help you after dinner."

"I got my work done at school, Mommy," Hannah replied as she picked up the plate and one of the glasses. Turning to her sister, she added, "I can help you with yours, if you want."

Morgan's heart swelled with pride at the selfless offer. Hannah was so patient with her twin, helping but never coddling, always asking permission rather than shoving in to do things for her. It wasn't easy parenting a child with such a profound challenge, but Hannah's fabulous attitude made it easier for Morgan.

"That's very sweet of you, honey," she approved, giving her a quick hug.

"Sweet," Allie echoed, lightly patting her sister's cheek, a faint, absent smile passing over her features as she turned away. Their interactions were often like that, but it was more than Allie could manage with most people. The doctors told Morgan the passing touches were a good sign that she was starting to overcome her inherent timidity and making progress into a more normal mode of interacting with others. Every day, usually more than once, Morgan prayed that they were right.

Once the girls were gone, Jessie dropped on her like a hawk. "How can Dad sit out there, chatting with Ty like nothing's ever gone wrong between you two?"

Truth be told, Morgan was just as baffled by his reaction to their old neighbor as her sister was. "It was a long time ago, and Dad always liked Ty. I guess he figures it's best to let bygones be bygones."

She didn't add the detail that Ty had apologized to her in town earlier. She wasn't sure why, but she wasn't quite ready to share that information just yet. Maybe she didn't believe him, or maybe it was the stubborn cowgirl in her, she mused, wanting to prolong his suffering awhile longer. Yeah, that was it.

"Well, I can hardly stand to look at him," Jessie announced, angling her head for a peek out the front window that looked onto the corner of the porch where Ty was sitting. Her gaze lingered there for several moments, and Morgan laughed.

"Right. There's not a woman alive who can resist that arrogant piece of work." She was living proof of that, she added silently.

"Handsome on the outside doesn't mean much when you've got a mean heart."

It was so simple for her, Morgan thought while she opened the closet in the back hall and pulled her leather barn gloves from the organizer. When you were twenty-four like

Jessie, the world was still painted in black and white, and things were either right or wrong. When you got older, those extra years taught you that there was a lot of gray out there.

"Anyway, I've got work to do outside. If you're leaving before I get back, have a good night."

"I'm doing laundry, so I'll be here awhile. Dinner will be in the oven keeping warm, just like always," Jessie said, as if she hadn't heard a word Morgan had said. "If you're out past seven, Dad and I will get the girls ready for bed and you can tuck them in when you come back."

Stopping by the back door, Morgan looked back and smiled. "Thanks, Jess. I don't know how I'd manage all this without you."

"Like Wonder Woman, of course." Her delighted expression made it clear that she appreciated the praise, and she blew Morgan a kiss before picking up one of her overstuffed laundry bags and heading down into the basement.

On the back porch, Morgan heard the sound of a truck's engine starting and glanced over to see Ty driving toward the road. Encountering him again had been more of a shock than she'd like to admit, but she forced her mind away from that prickly topic as she climbed into her 4x4 and went in the other direction. The front stock barn was her destination, and once she got there, a solid hour of unloading supplies and mucking stalls gave her a chance to settle her nerves and forget she'd seen the wayward rodeo star.

Almost.

Good-looking as ever, he still had the same quick smile that had gotten her attention when he was the new kid in class. A simple trick of the alphabet seated him behind her, and she'd endured chair kicking, braid pulling and outright aggravation for two weeks until she'd finally had enough and slugged him on the playground.

The incident had landed her in the principal's office, but it had earned her Ty's respect. From then on, she and their neighbor's youngest son had been thick as thieves. Sweethearts from high school to the rodeo circuit, they'd seemed on the road to a lifetime of good-natured arguments and the kind of love she'd always longed for.

And then, something happened. She still wasn't sure what had driven him to run away, and after many sleepless nights, she'd accepted the fact that she might never know. Well, mostly.

That thought had just floated through her

mind when she heard the sound of spitting gravel outside, followed by the slamming of a vehicle's door. Glancing out, she saw the object of her musings stalking toward her, looking fit to be tied.

"Something you wanna tell me, MJ?"

She hadn't heard the shorthand version of her full name in so long, it caught her by surprise. Recovering a bit, she narrowed her eyes and glared back at him. "I thought *goodbye* pretty much covered it."

"They're mine, aren't they?"

Morgan's heart stopped.

Realizing that the pitchfork she held was shaking in her hands, she carefully set it aside to give herself time to think. After drawing in a deep breath to settle her runaway blood pressure, she turned to him and summoned her best blank expression. "What are yours?"

"Allie and Hannah," he clarified, in a tone that told her in no uncertain terms that he knew she was stalling. "They're my daughters, aren't they?"

How could he possibly have figured that out? she wondered in a panic. They looked just like her, so she'd never confessed their father's identity to anyone. Not even her family.

"No, Ty, they're *my* daughters." Tapping

her chest for emphasis, she went on. "They're Whittakers, end of story."

Folding his arms, he scowled down at her but didn't say anything more. Then, in a matter of a few seconds, his demeanor shifted, and he grimaced as if she'd sucker punched him.

"Why didn't you tell me?" he asked in a quiet voice laced with regret. "I know we weren't in touch after I left, but you knew enough people who could've told you where I was."

"I didn't think you'd be interested," she shot back, clinging to her anger like a shield. "And while we're on it, you walked out on me with no explanation, no forwarding address. Once you pulled that stunt, I didn't think you were exactly father material."

He absorbed that in silence, a woeful look settling into an expression she'd never noticed on him in all the years they'd known each other. They'd been through hard stuff together, but he'd always been the lighthearted one, shrugging off things that would have caused a lesser man to stumble. Until the day he took off, she'd always believed that he could handle anything life threw at him without even breaking stride.

Gazing out the door toward the house, he

came back to her with the firm jaw she recalled so well. "I would've found a way to make it work for us, you know that. You never even gave me a chance."

She had to acknowledge that he was right, and the twinge of guilt she felt grew more insistent even as she tried to reason it away. "I made the best choice I could at the time."

"I know you did." Compassion softened his features, and she braced herself for the question she'd known he'd ask her at some point. "I don't understand how Hannah's so bright and Allie has autism. How does that kinda thing happen?"

"It's not anything I did while I was pregnant," Morgan informed him sternly, her back going up instantly. She'd told herself that over and over. But the nagging fear that she'd somehow caused her daughter's condition still haunted her, although she insisted otherwise. "As soon as I found out I was pregnant, I quit riding and came home. I was on bed rest for the last four months, doing absolutely nothing except making sure my babies had the best chance of being born healthy."

"Of course you did," he said gently, regret flooding his eyes. "I didn't mean to suggest you did anything wrong. I'm just wondering how one twin is totally normal and the other is left fighting such a huge challenge."

Morgan noticed that he didn't refer to Allie by her disability. It was something they'd all learned to do, because autism was a condition, not an identity. It was a subtle distinction to make, but an important one for the family. That he'd done it instinctively made her feel more inclined to cut him some slack. At least where the girls were concerned, she amended.

"Normal for Allie is different, that's all. Her abilities are different, too, but she makes the most of them. She's at the top of all her special classes, and like Dad told you, she has a great touch with animals. Socializing is tough for her, but she has a couple of classmates who she really likes hanging out with. Hannah and her friends are great with all of them, so they have a nice circle of girls together."

"How have you managed all this?" he asked, motioning around them at their surroundings, "and raising two kids by yourself?"

Admiration softened his eyes, giving her jangling nerves a much-needed boost. "Plenty of help, and a large helping of faith. I accept that God sent Allie to us for a reason, and I just keep doing my best."

The spark she'd noticed dimmed considerably, and he frowned. "You always had more faith than I did."

"It's a good thing, because I've needed every ounce of it."

He took that in with a pensive look. "Does it make things easier?"

"It makes them possible," she replied, opening up to him in a way she never could have imagined earlier. But part of him was reaching out to her, begging for understanding. Of what, she couldn't say, but it was tough to resist that plea from someone she'd loved for most of her life.

And then, she heard herself say, "Ty, I know there's something you're not telling me. What happened to bring you home this way?"

Frowning, he motioned her to a nearby bale of wood shavings. As he sat beside her, for the first time she noticed that his once-fluid movements had a labored look to them. Resting his hands on the knees of his expertly ripped designer jeans, he took a few moments to collect himself before starting. "Last year at an event in Oregon, I got tossed coming outta the chute. The bull was still fresh and had a good head of steam, and he decided throwing me wasn't enough. Long story short, he kicked me around that arena like a rag doll, and before the clowns could draw him away, he broke my back."

And his pride, she added silently. Anyone who'd known him before the accident could see that. "Oh, Ty, that's awful. He could've killed you."

"Yeah, I know," he admitted, swallowing hard before going on. "Anyway, I was in the hospital and rehab a long time, and even with my insurance, it got pretty expensive." Nodding out to the truck, he added, "I've had to sell everything except that and Clyde. As of tomorrow, the truck belongs to a guy who lives over in Pine Valley. So it's just me and Clyde and the five acres I bought from my parents when they sold their place a few years ago."

"What are you gonna do?"

"Not sure," he admitted soberly. "Preferably something that won't cripple me."

Tyler Wilkins had never been renowned for his brains, and physical work was clearly out of the picture for him now. That didn't leave many options for him around a small town like Mustang Ridge. "Such as?"

"Not sure," he repeated, adding a wry grin. "Guess I should've paid more attention in math class."

"And science, social studies, English." She

added a few more of his less successful academic subjects through the years, ticking them off on her fingers.

"Yeah, well, you were always the smart one."

"I never should've let you copy off me. You would've learned more that way."

"No, I'd still be in high school, trying to figure out why the guy who invented algebra thought that mixing letters and numbers was a good idea."

She laughed at that, and when he joined her, it struck her as odd to be sitting here in the barn, sharing a humorous moment with the man she'd once vowed to never speak to again. She hadn't forgiven him, but she also couldn't bring herself to keep kicking him when he was so far down he might not claw his way back to what he used to be for a long time. If ever.

"So," he ventured in a hesitant voice, "does this mean you don't hate me anymore?"

She didn't answer him right away, as if she had to think it over. They were still there on that bale, mutely staring at each other, when her younger brother Ryan appeared in the open doorway at the other end of the barn.

"What's goin' on in here?" he demanded, clearly alarmed by what he saw. Hurrying over to stand in front of them, he planted his hands on his hips as he faced Ty in a protective stance. "Whatever you're doing here, it looks to me like you're done. It'd be good for you to leave before I forget we used to be friends."

"I'm not here to make trouble," Ty explained, his reasonable tone another surprise from the formerly hotheaded cowboy she recalled. "Morgan and I have something to talk about."

"Not anymore, you don't. You wanna talk to her, use a phone." Ryan took another step forward and growled, "Now, get out."

Ty didn't protest further, but he did tip his hat to her on his way out. The faint smile he gave her was a pale imitation of the one she'd treasured in the past, and despite the jolt he'd given her, she couldn't help feeling sorry for him. He'd tumbled a long way down from the peak of his spectacular life, and it seemed that he was in for a long, hard recovery.

Then, in a flash of insight, she understood why her brother had rushed to her defense when he—like everyone else—knew she was perfectly capable of taking care of herself. "How much did you hear?"

"More than I think you'd like." Grimacing, he added, "Then again, I figured it out for myself about ten minutes after you came home to tell Dad you were pregnant."

That was news to her, and her heart plummeted to the floor. "How? I was eight weeks along, and Ty was long gone. Anyone could've been the father."

"Come on, sis," he chided, shaking his head. "You might've fooled everyone else, but I know you. It was Ty. It was always Ty."

Yes, it was, she conceded as he strolled off and left her alone in the barn. But for the past seven years, she'd been focused solely on raising her girls and doing everything in her power to keep their legacy ranch in the black. Then the threat of development had pushed her to start the conservancy, which gobbled up most of her precious spare time. By necessity, she'd put aside her past failings and turned all of her effort toward making the future the best it could possibly be for her daughters.

Because, quite honestly, the only other option was to give up. And no matter how long the odds were, a Whittaker never, ever quit.

That thought had just rolled through her head when her cell phone rang. She didn't recognize the number, so she answered with, "Whittaker Ranch, this is Morgan."

"Hey there, cowgirl." A sigh escaped her

before she could stop it, and Ty chuckled. "Not who you were expecting, huh?"

"How did you get this number?"

"Found it on the ranch's website. Nice job with that, by the way."

"Jessie's in charge of that stuff, so I'll pass on the compliment. What do you want?"

"We weren't exactly done talking when Sheriff Ryan showed up and ran me off," Ty pointed out, his tone as casual as if they'd been discussing the next livestock auction on the schedule.

"I was."

Her terse response seemed to catch him off guard, because there was a quiet hum on the line while he absorbed that one. "Well, I wasn't. I just found out I have two daughters, and I've got some more questions."

"Such as?"

"I'd really rather hash this out in person."

She'd really rather never see him again, but apparently that wasn't going to happen. They'd have to hammer out some kind of compromise eventually, so she relented. "Fine. When and where?"

"I've got stuff going on the next couple days, so I was thinking my place Friday night, after you get the girls tucked in. I'll be around, so come over whenever it works for you."

"It doesn't work for me anytime," she spat before realizing that he'd already hung up. Thumbing her phone off, she glared at it and slid it into the back pocket of her jeans.

An evening alone with Tyler Wilkins, she mused while she slit open another bale of shavings and began shoveling the contents into a wheelbarrow. There were plenty of women who'd kill to be in her boots right now.

Too bad she wasn't one of them.

To Ty's knowledge, there wasn't a word for how bad the cabin smelled.

His concerns about rodents had turned out to be right, but he hadn't counted on there being so many corpses scattered around. Opening all the windows had helped a little, but he was going to need some heavy-duty cleaner and a good measure of patience to rid the house of the smell entirely. Fortunately for him, there weren't any storms in the forecast for the next week, so he should be able to air it out in a few days.

For the past couple of days, he'd been relegated to being outside, cleaning up years' worth of fallen limbs and rotting leaves. Behind him, he heard a mellow nicker and said, "Not now, Clyde. I know you're antsy, but I've got a ton of stuff to do today. We'll take a ride tomorrow."

"How 'bout now?"

Startled by the sound of another voice, Ty whipped around to find Morgan and Sadie trotting up the grassy aisle that separated his property from the Whittaker place. Setting aside his rake, he strolled over to greet them. "And here I thought he was talking to me. Weren't we meeting up on Friday?"

"I don't get out as much as I'd like these days, so I was going to ride out and watch the sunset anyway. If you want to come along, we can talk on the way."

Translation—I don't want to give you home field advantage. She was the only woman he'd ever known who strategized that way, and it was comforting to know she hadn't lost that sharp quality over the years.

It was also more than a little intimidating, he mused as he quickly tacked up and hauled himself into the saddle. She'd always been smarter than him, and chances were the gap hadn't closed up enough to make much difference. He'd do well to remember that.

The horses were old friends, and the two of them traded looks occasionally while they trotted companionably side by side, as if they'd last seen each other earlier that week instead of seven years ago. Morgan seemed content to ride in silence, and Ty followed her lead, taking the opportunity to reacquaint himself with his surroundings.

Wild prairie and barely tamed pastureland stretched out like a quilt of grass and flowers for miles around them. Ringed by thick stands of pines, the broad valley was cut through by the winding currents of the Calico River. Modest in width but dependable even in the driest years, the deep-running mountain stream supplied the local ranches with a reliable source of water for their livestock.

Beyond that rose the majestic Bridger Mountains, which ran along the northern boundaries of Mustang Ridge and several other small towns nearby. Home to everything from mountain lions to grizzlies to bighorn sheep, those ragged peaks were the image that always came into Ty's head when he thought of home.

As he and Morgan gained altitude, they got an ever-broader perspective of the valley below. When a small herd of horses came into view, he asked, "Where did they come from?"

"Everywhere. A few years ago, the state took an interest in our mustangs and managing the population. I didn't like their solution, so I stepped in and petitioned to adopt the herd." Gazing over at the milling animals, her face softened with affection for the creatures she'd managed to save. Pointing, she explained, "Over there is public land available to anyone for open grazing, and the strip with access to the river belongs to a local family. They gave me permission to use it, so I relocated the ponies and started a mustang rescue. I break and train some of them for people who want to use them as pleasure horses, but the others stay here, where they belong."

Her very practical approach to the problem didn't surprise him in the least, but he was impressed all the same. "That's awesome. Not many folks would go to that much trouble for some wild ponies."

"They're the symbol of everything the Mustang Ridge Conservancy stands for," she told him firmly, her jaw set in determination. "If the animals who've always lived here lose their birthright, chances are we won't be far behind."

When Sadie and Clyde reached the southern bank of the creek, Morgan finally stopped and turned to him. Her eyes held a resigned look that he tried not to take personally.

Letting Sadie drop her head for a drink, Morgan said, "So, you wanted to talk."

"Can we get down first? My back's not as limber as it used to be." Plus, he didn't want her taking off if she didn't like something he said. Clyde was a gamer, but there was no way he could catch the half-mustang mare at a full run.

"Fine."

Swinging down, she led Sadie to a nearby clump of elms and tied her reins to a branch to let her graze. Ty did the same and then joined Morgan on a fallen log near the creek.

When he noticed her pained expression, he asked, "Something wrong?"

"You weren't exaggerating about your back, were you?"

"Nope. I've got a bunch of fused vertebrae and a doctor's warning to never get on another horse for the rest of my life."

"But you're still riding?" Giving him a hard look, she shook her head. "That's crazy."

"Maybe, but Clyde's as safe as one of those carousel horses kids ride on at the fair. Besides, life's too short to be afraid of things that *might* happen. When you've had the misfortunes I have, you learn to appreciate what's left."

That got him a nod, which he took as a

tacit sign of acceptance, if not understanding. They sat for a while, trading small talk while they admired the gradually sinking sun as it began its nightly descent over the mountains. He recognized that she had children to get home to, and he moved on to the subject he'd insisted they discuss.

"Morgan." When he had her attention, he summoned his courage and forged ahead. "I want to help out with Allie and Hannah. You've carried all the weight for long enough, and I'm ready to take on my share."

That got him a derisive snort. "I doubt it."

Reaching into his back pocket, he pulled out a folded paper and handed it to her. "I'm serious. Maybe this'll convince you I mean what I'm saying."

She carefully took the certified check from him as if it was a rattlesnake coiled to strike and opened it with a wary expression. When she saw the amount, her mouth fell into a shocked O, and those gorgeous blue eyes met his in astonishment. "This is a lot of money."

"Delivered my truck to the new owner the other day," he explained, feeling proud of himself for the first time in ages. "I found a used one cheaper than I expected, so the rest is for you and the girls. I talked to a lawyer buddy of mine and found out that six years of child support for two kids adds up to a lot. This is a down payment. Once I get myself sorted out, he'll help us come up with a permanent arrangement so you won't have to worry about money anymore."

"Thank you," she murmured, clearly stunned by the offer. "I never would've expected this, Ty. It's very generous of you."

It was, which was what he'd been counting on when he devised a plan for approaching this very independent woman about their daughters. Having offered his help, he now moved on to what he considered to be the more important element of his proposal.

"It's my responsibility, as their father," he ventured cautiously, watching her for any sign of disagreement. When she didn't show one, he decided it was safe for him to continue. "It's also my responsibility to be a part of their lives. If they want me there."

"So this is a bribe?" she demanded, jamming the check into his chest with enough force to nearly knock him off the log. Shoving away from him, she jumped to her feet and scowled down at him. "Keep your money and your fake concern, Tyler Wilkins. My daughters and I have done just fine without you all these years, and we'll keep going that way long after you're gone."

This woman could still spike his temper into boiling range with a single look, but he summoned a calm tone as he got to his feet and matched her frosty look with one of his own. "I'm not going anywhere, MJ. First off, I've got nowhere else to go. And second— and more important—I intend to stick around so my daughters and I can get to know each other. I've missed the first six years of their lives, and I'm not gonna miss any more."

With that, he wheeled around and mounted Clyde as gracefully as he could. Reaching over, he tucked the check under the corner of Sadie's saddle blanket and headed toward home without a look back.

Let her stew over that one, he thought with a grin as he rode away. She wasn't the only one with a stubborn streak

Chapter Three

"Now, remember, Morgan," Dad cautioned her as he pulled into the parking lot at the high school. "This is our first meeting with this energy company rep, and it's bound to be a little nutsy. This is an important issue for everyone around here, not just us. You're gonna have to be patient with folks when they're trying to talk."

Morgan gave him the irritated look she reserved for people who had the gall to tell her how she was *supposed* to behave. "I know that, Dad. Please don't speak to me like I'm ten years old."

"You're real passionate about this, and I love that about you. But let's be honest— you've got a knack for taking over a situation, convinced you've got the answer to the problem. This is bigger than one or two families, and it's gonna take all of us to hammer out a solution everyone can live with."

"You know some of our neighbors are on the verge of selling out to that greedy shark, right?" He nodded, and she turned to face him squarely. "If they accept his offer, we might as well do the same thing, because in a couple years the Calico River will be liquid poison and our place will be downstream from an industrial complex that'll be churning out pollutants and noise twenty-four/seven."

"We're not gonna let that happen," he assured her, patting her shoulder in a calming gesture. "But we won't get anywhere by pressuring folks into seeing things our way. They've gotta come to the right decision on their own."

"I just can't believe anyone who's got half a brain would want to ruin all that," she grumbled, staring out the dusty windshield of his truck at the expanse of the oddly named Crazy Mountains to the north. "That's some of God's best handiwork out there, and it's up to us to keep it that way."

"Preaching to the choir."

"I know. I'm just more frustrated than usual, I guess." She blew out an exasperated breath to cool her temper. It helped, but not enough. She recognized that was because she now had a new problem to contend with— namely Ty Wilkins—and she didn't know what she was going to do about it.

Heaving a sigh of his own, Dad got out and circled the old SUV to open her door for her the way he'd done since she was a child. "Stick with comments about God's handiwork in there, and you'll get a lot further than if you get into a shouting match with people who're on the fence about land development."

"Okay," she agreed grudgingly. "You make a good point."

"Flies and honey, sweetheart."

Diplomacy wasn't exactly her strong point, Morgan groused silently as they went up the wide front steps into the school. But the Mustang Ridge Conservancy was fighting for the very existence that generations of Whittakers had worked so hard to create. She wanted Allie and Hannah to grow up surrounded by the same view she'd loved from the time she could appreciate it. If the only way to make that happen was muting her characteristic drive, she'd just have to figure out a way to do it.

Inside, the auditorium was packed. Up on the stage that normally hosted student concerts and plays, there was a long table and several chairs. A man she didn't recognize was talking with Kevin Carmichael, the town's only dentist and their newly elected mayor. He was the developer everyone had been buzzing about the past few weeks, judging by his tailored suit and polished appearance.

Her father had artfully intercepted the man when he visited their ranch, respectfully hearing him out before sending him on his way. Mostly because he knew perfectly well that if the stranger had found Morgan first, she would have blown a gasket before throwing him off the property. Her beloved mustangs had nowhere else to go, and if the Whittakers lost their right to use the open rangeland where the wild ponies roamed, they'd be rounded up and sent to some random place where she wouldn't be able to help them. The only way to save them was to get that land legally protected as wilderness forever. It was a tall order, even for a woman who'd never run from a challenge in her life.

"Hey, Morgan." Hearing her name, she turned to find Dave Farley sitting behind her. "Any of those mustang yearlings ready to go yet?"

"A couple. What are you looking for?"

"An Appaloosa. A friend of mine in Billings just lost her mare after twenty-plus years and is looking for a youngster to take in. I told her about your rescue outfit, and she's interested in meeting you."

Finally, some good news, Morgan thought, smiling as she fished a card out of her purse. "Tell her she can call me anytime. I've got an App who should be green broke sometime this summer, if that works for her. If she sends me her info, I'll take some pics and email them to her. He's gorgeous, and the vet says he should top out around fifteen hands."

"That's tall for a wild one."

"His daddy's a big, strapping stallion," she explained, feeling a jolt of pride that her small herd of wild horses and rescues was doing so well. "I'll send your friend some photos of the sire and dam, too."

"Thanks. I'll let her know."

He sat back, then stood and grinned at someone behind Morgan. "Hey, Ty," he greeted their prodigal cowboy, offering his hand. "Welcome home."

"Thanks, Dave. It's good to see you. How're Bonnie and the boys?"

"Good, busy. They're both playing baseball this year, so she's at their game tonight." The proud father held up his phone. "She's keeping me updated by text."

"Great idea. Tell her I said hi."

"Will do."

Dave sat and started typing on his phone while Ty looked down at Morgan. "Mind if I take this seat?"

She shrugged. "It's a free country."

The moron actually had the audacity to grin at that, and once he was settled, he leaned in to say, "I'm not the enemy, MJ."

"Y'know," she shot back, her already unsettled nerves tightening like the over-stretched strings of a fiddle. "No one calls me that anymore."

"Yeah?" The grin widened, and he draped a muscled forearm over the back of his chair. "Then I guess that makes me special."

Dad chuckled beside her, and she angled a look at him. "You think that's funny?"

"Yup. You two are as entertaining as ever."

"I'm so glad you're amused by your daughter being harassed."

"How's Clyde settling into your new place?" he asked, pointedly looking over her head at Ty.

"Fine. He's used to moving around, so being in a new barn doesn't bother him a bit. The house, well, that's a different story."

Dad chuckled again. "Oily rags and a match might be your best option."

"I'll keep that in mind."

The two of them carried on that way, talking over the top of her as if she wasn't even there, until Kevin called the meeting to order.

"Okay, folks, let's all take our seats." Once everyone was settled, he gripped the lectern in both hands as if he was preparing for a long, difficult night. "Since we all know why we're here tonight, I'd like to turn the stage over to Mr. Reynolds, a representative of Cartwright Energy. They're the outfit from Utah that's interested in prospecting for oil and natural gas on the wild lands north of town, and he's here to make a presentation about their proposal. After that, he'll answer any questions you might have about their operation."

Morgan had read the prospectus cover to cover—three times—so she knew what it contained. After several hours of discouraging research, she had a pretty good idea what they were up against. While she half listened to the slick performance unfolding up on stage, she kept a roving eye on the assembly to gauge their neighbors' reactions to what they were hearing. Some looked intrigued, others were obviously fuming, but most seemed to be neutral.

At least for now.

Those who hadn't yet made up their minds were the ones who gave her hope that their efforts to protect the ridge from development might actually have a chance at succeeding. When the man was finished, several people asked the usual questions about land values and potential for damaging the local environment. All of them were deftly handled by their guest, who clearly had a lot of practice dealing with local residents' apprehension about his company's activities.

When the comments dwindled into silence, Kevin stood to take his place at the lectern. "Thank you for coming, Mr. Reynolds. I'm sure we'll be talking to each other again real soon."

Their polite handshake was punctuated by equally polite applause, and the executive gathered up his materials and his designer briefcase and strolled out. His confident gait suggested to Morgan that he thought the presentation had gone well.

"He thinks we're a bunch of uneducated hicks," Ty muttered in unbridled disgust. "Just 'cause you've got graphs and stuff on a fancy laptop don't mean that what you're planning to do is okay. Anyone with half a brain can see that what they're proposing is gonna destroy everything within thirty miles of that installation."

Stunned by his quick—and very accurate—assessment, she stared at him in disbelief. "You really think that?"

"I'm not the sharpest knife in the drawer, but I know a song and dance when I see one. The front office executives sent this guy to pull the wool over our eyes, but I got news for him. We ain't sheep."

"All right, folks," the mayor announced, rubbing his hands together in anticipation. "What do we think?"

That was a mistake, Morgan thought wryly, as the general hum of comments escalated into a chaotic mess. After waiting a couple of minutes for the hubbub to die down, Kevin apparently decided it wasn't going to happen anytime soon. Pleading for cooperation, he managed to regain control of the restless crowd and plucked his microphone from its stand. Handing it off to the town clerk, he said, "Polly, take this around to people who've got something to say. That way, we can all hear what's going on for ourselves."

"My place isn't big, but it's up near the ridge," one elderly man said, "and they're offering us triple what it was assessed for last fall. My wife and I are barely scraping by on our fixed income, and we can't hardly afford the taxes anymore. We've got no choice but to sell."

Unable to sit still any longer, Morgan jumped to her feet. "Anyone who's got land to sell, the Mustang Ridge Conservancy is interested in buying. We don't have the kind of money Cartwright does, but we'll work with you to find an arrangement that suits all of us. We can't just let them stroll through here and destroy anything that's in the way of profits that may or may not be buried under our land."

Her offer got everyone buzzing again, and Kevin had a tough time getting the meeting back under control. Several people voiced their support of the conservancy, while others scoffed at it as a waste of time and effort.

"Standing in the way of progress is pointless," one woman insisted. "If it doesn't happen now, sometime in the future it will."

"Not while I'm around and still breathing," Dad assured her in his booming, listen-to-me voice as he got to his feet beside Morgan. "My family dug our homestead outta the dirt with their bare hands back in 1882, and we've got no intention of letting it go now. Or ever."

Many sitting around them voiced their agreement, and the public debate got side-

tracked into a multitude of conversations between friends and neighbors over what to do
and the best way to go about getting it done.

In the middle of it all, Ty leaned in close
and said, "Way to go, cowgirl."

When she looked at him, he grinned and
gave her the same wink he'd used when they
were kids planning some kind of mischief.
And for the first time since he'd so unexpectedly strolled back into her life, she felt herself wanting to smile back. But that would
only encourage him, so she stemmed the impulse and returned her attention to the meeting. There was the expected back-and-forth,
and at the end the only thing that had changed
was that they were all an hour older.

She was by nature a decisive person, so the
hemming and hawing grated on her nerves.
Her father, on the other hand, seemed to take
it all in stride, even hanging back to chat with
people when the official gathering had been
called to a close. Long past the end of her patience already, she opted to scoot out a side
door and wait for him outside.

To her annoyance, Ty trailed after her. He
didn't say anything, but just having him next
to her was both a distraction and an annoyance. He'd picked up a new cologne, she noticed even though she was supposed to be

beyond registering that kind of thing about the man she'd come to think of as the runaway cowboy. The scent had a campfire, leathery quality to it, and she grudgingly admitted that it suited him well.

But there was no way she was telling him that. Instead, she folded her arms and scowled up at him. "What do you want?"

He grinned back, and she braced herself for what was coming next. In a million years, she never could have predicted what she heard.

"Y'know, I always did admire your spunk." Leaning back against the tree behind him, he went on. "I also admire the way you have with animals. Instinctive, like you know what they're thinking. Whether it's training a new horse or herding calves, you're always a step or two ahead of 'em so you can head 'em off before they get into trouble."

"That's all well and good, but what does any of that have to do with the meeting?"

"And then there's that laser focus of yours," he added with a chuckle. "The thing is, when your eyes are on the prize, sometimes you miss things that are fanned out to the sides."

"Such as?"

In answer, he pulled out his phone and scrolled down the contact list to the name he thought might interest her. He handed it over, and when she took in the name, her eyes widened as they met his. "You know Congressman Barlowe?"

"Turns out Craig's a big rodeo fan. We've had dinner a few times, and he strikes me as a good guy who really cares about protecting Montana's natural treasures. I think the conservancy would be something he'd want to know about."

"I've written a dozen letters to him," Morgan confided in a dejected tone very unlike the feisty cowgirl he used to know. "I always get a form response that basically says he's a busy man with a lot to do, so we'll have to get in line behind everyone else."

"How many folks are in the group so far?" She hesitated, and he said, "Let me guess. You and JD."

"And some others." He gave her a nudging look, and she relented with a sigh. "Okay, there's six of us so far. This energy company's only been here a couple times, and most people don't see any harm in them hand-drilling for soil and core samples. The trouble is, if they find something, the bulldozers and excavators will be here within a few weeks. Once they have permits and geological surveys that tell them where to start prospecting, it might be too late for us to stop them."

Still the smartest kid in the room, he thought. "Sounds like you've done your homework."

"You have no idea. This kind of thing goes on all the time, and in places where the residents don't have the will or organization to put up some resistance, the big energy companies get what they want. I know the country needs to find more sources of oil and natural gas, but there must be better ways to do it."

"I don't doubt that, but it'll take some really smart folks working together to make that happen."

"That's what the conservancy is all about. We just need more members." After a pause, she frowned. "A lot more."

He hated seeing her so dejected. He much preferred the in-your-face attitude she'd had earlier, even if it made him a target every once in a while. Fortunately, he held the key to lifting her spirits this time, and it felt great.

"You also need a bigwig who can help bring the right kind of attention to your cause." Ty rocked his phone side to side. "Wanna meet your congressman?"

"Yes," she replied without even a hint of

trepidation. "You convince him to visit Mustang Ridge, and I'll take it from there."

He almost agreed, then realized there was a golden opportunity for him in this. It might be his only chance to mend fences with her, and he couldn't let it slip by without at least giving it a shot. "Not so fast. Craig and I are friends, and he'll be staying at my place while he's here. I'm not just gonna make introductions and step away. I wanna be involved in the conservancy and what it's trying to do."

Those gorgeous blue eyes narrowed into glittering slits. "Why? You never cared about stuff like that before."

"I do now. I want our daughters to grow up the way we did, in a wild place with plenty of fresh air and open space. Not choking on the pollution from a bunch o' gas and oil rigs."

He knew she wouldn't accept his help on its own merit alone, but reminding her of one of her own reasons for doing this might persuade her to take him on despite their rocky history.

The front doors banged open, and several people flooded out, still arguing about what to do. JD was among them, and he detoured away from the group to join Morgan and Ty.

"Ready to go?" he asked his daughter.

Clearly thinking about what Ty had said,

she hesitated and then nodded. "Yeah." Connecting with Ty again, she gave him a wry grin that told him she wasn't thrilled with his proposal but recognized that it made sense. "So, call your politician buddy and set up a visit. You and I can take him around and show him how beautiful this area is and let him see for himself why it's worth saving."

Thrilled with her approval of his plan— however reluctant it might be—he barely held back a triumphant whoop. Instead, he grinned and nodded. "Will do."

"And you can stop being all grown-up," she teased, the grin shifting to a slightly warmer version. "I know you're dying to go all yee-hah on me."

"Well, now, that'd be immature. I'll wait till I'm in my truck."

That got him a short laugh, and she walked away with JD, shaking her head. Ty watched her go, and for the first time in months, he felt as if things might finally be shifting to go his way.

What she'd given him wasn't exactly the *I forgive you* that he was hoping for. But it was a start.

Chapter Four

"That drawing of Teddy looks great, Allie," Morgan approved, patting her budding nature artist lightly on the shoulder. Her daughter still wasn't fond of too much physical contact, but with the family exercising a lot of patience and gentle persistence, she was getting better at accepting it from people she knew well. Morgan hated forcing the gestures on her, but the occupational therapist had assured them that tolerating some tactile interaction was an important part of Allie learning how to function in the world outside her own home. And since the goal was to encourage her to be as independent as possible, they all kept doing it.

"Thank you," her shy girl replied, adding a rare smile. "I think he had fun."

As rewarding as the smile had been, her

two-stage response made Morgan's heart swell with pride. Bolstered by a fabulous teaching team in her special-needs classroom and plenty of good, old-fashioned prayer, Allie had come so far in the past year. While Morgan knew there was a lifetime of challenges ahead for her beautiful daughter, moments like this one gave her hope for the future.

And then, Allie surprised her again. Looking across the table at her twin, she said, "Hannah helped me with math. I get it now."

Glancing up from her workbook, Hannah beamed. "That's really nice, but you did the hard part. You're way better at numbers than you think you are."

Allie didn't respond to that, but a faint dimple showed in her cheek as she fished around in the multicolored box of artist's pencils and crayons Jessie had given her last Christmas. Morgan wanted to crush them both in a grateful Mom hug but out of respect for Allie, she settled for dropping a quick kiss on top of each curly ponytail. "When you girls are done, go up and brush your teeth and get into your jammies. Then we'll cuddle in my room and watch your princess spy show until bedtime. Okay?"

"Awesome!" Hannah exclaimed, adding a bright smile. "There's two new ones on tonight."

"Yeah, I seem to remember hearing something about that," Morgan teased on her way out of the kitchen. "I have to talk to Grandpa about a few things, but I'll be up soon."

"Okay, Mommy."

After a couple of seconds, Allie echoed the response. She didn't look up from her picture, but getting any reaction at all was a big deal, and Morgan was still smiling about it when she knocked on the half-open door of her father's den.

"Come in!"

She found him surrounded by a sea of paperwork, a good portion of which was buried under Matilda, the largest cat any of them had ever seen. She looked like a cross between a Persian and a bobcat, and she lolled her head to the side to watch Morgan cross the scarred pine floor. At one time, this space had been the sum total of the Whittaker homestead cabin, a single room that had housed Elijah, his wife, Charlotte, and their four children. And when the wolves were running around unchecked, sometimes even a new calf or two.

How they did it, she really couldn't imagine. But she was grateful to them and determined settlers like them who'd had the guts to stick it out and pass the land along to their descendants. Now it was her responsibility to take good care of the property and hand it down the line, and she took that duty very seriously.

Curling up in an oversize leather chair, she waited for her dad to finish the line he was reading and glance over the top of a pair of bifocals that looked as if they'd been worn by Ben Franklin himself. "Are we sure this stuff is written in English?"

Morgan laughed at the sour look on his weather-beaten face. "Lawyer's English. That's why I think we need one, before the conservancy drowns in an avalanche of government forms. Jessie's gonna talk to her new boss and see if Brooke will help us out."

That soured his look even more. "She's a kid fresh out of law school. What does she know?"

"New lawyers are eager to prove themselves," she reasoned. "Plus, they tend to be idealistic, which means she might work for a lower fee. Or even for nothing, if Jessie bribes her with a few homemade goodies. She has a way with people."

A quality Morgan envied, she admitted silently. Being the youngest, Jessie had always had the freedom to be lighthearted and sweet. Their brother Ben did his own thing, running the crop section of the ranch, and Ryan was a tough but fair wrangler in charge of the cowboys who came and went with the seasons.

That left JD and Morgan the task of working and overseeing the ranch as a whole. Since she was the oldest, she supposed that it made sense. But there were times when she sensed that their customers would rather deal with Ryan or Ben than a woman. Those were the times when she gritted her teeth, plastered on a beauty queen smile and plowed through what needed to be done as quickly as possible.

"Unlike you, you mean?" Dad commented, echoing her thoughts with unnerving accuracy.

"Well, schmoozing people's not my thing. I prefer animals."

He glanced from right to left, as if looking for spies. Then he leaned forward and muttered, "Yeah, me, too."

Morgan laughed, and as he leaned back in his chair, Matilda padded across the wide desktop and plopped into his lap. Smiling, he stroked her silky fur and went on. "Critters are easier to understand. You feed 'em a couple times a day, keep the water trough full, brush 'em if they need it. Give 'em some attention, and they're happy."

His humorous tone had shifted to a melancholy one, and Morgan eyed him in concern. "That doesn't sound like you. Is something wrong?"

"Nah, just tired." She kept the look going, and he relented with a sigh. "It's been tough since we lost your mother last year."

"We didn't lose her, Dad," Morgan reminded him firmly, hoping to nip his misplaced sorrow in the bud. "She's living in Helena to be near her boyfriend."

He absorbed that in silence, then sighed again. "You think she's happy?"

"I haven't heard from her, so I wouldn't know." Didn't much care, either, but that was another issue. As beautiful as she was narcissistic, Laura Whittaker might have birthed four children, but as a mother she was a huge disappointment. Honestly, it was a blessing that they'd all turned out so well.

"Me, neither." He grimaced, and Matilda reached a paw up to his cheek as if she sensed that he needed some feline comforting. He snuck a finger under her chin and rubbed the spot that made her rumble like a fine sports car. Chuckling, he looked over at Morgan. "See? Easy to please."

"Unlike the legal system," she added, nodding at the stacks of paper he'd printed. "Please tell me that's research and not the application package we have to file to get our injunction against Cartwright."

"Some of each. It's easier to read it this way than on the computer. But I gotta admit, there's plenty of groups in other states fighting the same thing we are. Jessie showed me how to navigate their websites, and I'm hoping to get some hints from their message boards."

"That's a great idea," Morgan agreed, suddenly feeling more optimistic about their battle than she had been since the incredibly unproductive town meeting. "Maybe we can connect with some of these other organizations and get recommendations from them on what to do or not to do. It could save us a lot of time, which is something we don't have much of if we want to stop the exploration that shark Reynolds is proposing."

"What about Ty's congressman friend? When is he coming?"

"Well…" Morgan suddenly felt the way she used to as a child when her father asked if her chores were done and she had to tell him she hadn't even started yet. "He gave us a few dates that work for him, but I haven't followed up on that yet."

Her father's silvery-blue eyes squinted in disapproval. "Why not?"

Because it was Ty, and she hated asking him for anything. She still didn't trust him, and it made her skin crawl to think that the fate of Mustang Ridge hung at least partially on the integrity of the charming cowboy who'd broken her trust and her heart on his way out of her life. While she was trying to come up with a decent explanation, her father shook his head with an understanding smile.

"I know it's hard to put your past with him aside to work with him on this. But that was years ago, and the problems we have now are gonna need a lot of people to solve them. If he's willing to help, we have to take him up on his offer."

"I know."

After a moment, he cleared his throat in an obvious sign that he was about to get parental with her. But what he said next almost knocked her onto the floor.

"I know he's Allie and Hannah's father."

Morgan's jaw nearly hit the floor, and she stared at him in disbelief. "How?"

"Honey, I know you're all grown-up now,

but some things about you are the same as they always were. When you told us you were pregnant, I never doubted for a second that Ty was the father."

Once she'd recovered somewhat, she demanded, "Why didn't you say something?"

His shrug reminded her distinctly of Ryan. "It wasn't my place. I figured when you were ready, you'd tell me yourself. In the meantime, I'd just enjoy being the grandpa of the two sweetest girls in Montana."

"Do Jessie and Ben know?"

"Not from me, but it wouldn't surprise me if they do." The mantel clock chimed seven, and right on cue, Matilda jumped from his lap, trotting from the room to the kitchen, where her evening treats were. As he stood, his leathery features cracked into a grin. "You're many things, Morgan Jo, but deceitful ain't one of 'em. Some folks just aren't good at lying."

"You make that sound like a good thing."

"In my opinion, it is."

On his way past, he kissed the top of her head the way she'd done with her own daughters earlier. It made her feel like his little girl again, and she couldn't help smiling. Alone in the quiet room, she leaned her head back against the old leather and stared at the dusky landscape outside the window.

Enough waffling, she decided, pulling out her phone to find Ty's number. When he answered, she did her best to sound casual about the reason for her call. "Dad and I were talking, and we decided it's a good idea to firm things up with Craig. What do you need from me to make that happen?"

"Just your go-ahead," he assured her in a reliable tone that was very unlike the rakish cowboy she'd once adored. "You want him to visit any time in particular?"

"Yesterday."

Chuckling, he replied, "Got it. I'll see what I can do and get back to you."

"Good. And, Ty?"

"Yeah?"

Swallowing her pride, she decided it was best to finish her response before she could think better of it. "Thank you."

"Anytime."

After she hung up, she was struck by the thought that his final word had a nice, dependable ring to it. Almost as if a girl could count on him to step up and take care of things when she needed him to.

Of course, she knew better, she reminded herself as she headed upstairs for some cuddle time with her daughters and their favorite new show. She'd learned the hard way that Ty Wilkins wasn't to be trusted. She only prayed that he could manage to be responsible for long enough to help protect Mustang Ridge from the developers who were so keen on destroying it.

"So, how was the flight in from DC?" Ty asked while he and Craig Barlowe wound their way through the crowd clustered around the baggage carousels.

"Long," sighed the man who had the distinction of being the youngest member of Congress. "Fortunately for me, I'm new enough that no one outside Montana or Washington knows who I am. Pop in some earbuds, open a book and folks more or less leave me alone. Except for the kid behind me who kicked the back of my seat all the way in from Chicago."

Ty would rather drive across the entire country than be trapped in a cramped airplane, and he groaned in sympathy. "Man, I hate flying. I know it's quicker, but I always feel like I'm gonna lose my mind before I get to where I'm going. You're stacked up like rows of cordwood, and you don't get to see anything until you land."

They'd reached the airport's outer doors, and Craig paused on the sidewalk with a smile. Nodding at the distant mountain range, he said, "But when you do land, the view's incredible."

"You should take the train sometime. You'd see mile after mile of the best scenery in the world."

Craig snorted at the suggestion. "Are you kidding? I've got barely enough time to fly in and out of Helena these days. My assistant had to finagle like crazy to get me an overnight at your place. I haven't been home in six months," he added with a heavy sigh.

Ty recalled the rigors of keeping up with that kind of schedule only too well. "Yeah, the rodeo circuit was pretty demanding, too. I can relate."

"Don't get me wrong," Craig amended as they approached Ty's pickup. "I love what I do, and I'm grateful to get the opportunity to make life better for people. I just wish all this—" he motioned at the impressive surroundings "—wasn't so far from DC."

Setting his friend's bag behind the seat, Ty levered it back into place and climbed in. "If Mustang Ridge was any closer to civilization, it would've lost its appeal for me a long time ago."

"Good point." While Ty found his way out of the parking lot, Craig pulled out his phone and growled something under his breath. "What part of 'going off the grid' do these people not understand?"

Without a word, Ty held out his hand. At first, Craig looked confused, then got the unspoken comment and handed over the sleek handset. While they waited at the ticket booth to pay for parking, Ty powered the phone off and slid it into the back pocket of his jeans. "That oughta do it."

"I guess it will," Craig agreed with a chuckle. Leaning his head back against the seat, he closed his eyes with a grin. "Thanks."

"No problem."

He and the young politician weren't exactly longtime buddies, but Ty knew an exhausted person when he saw one. During the drive to Mustang Ridge, he kept quiet to let Craig relax for as long as he could. At one point, he heard light snoring, and he couldn't help grinning. *Better rest up now*, he thought as he turned off the highway and onto the two-lane road that led to the ranches outside the town limits. *Hurricane Morgan is waiting for you at the other end.*

They stopped at his place to unload Craig's bag and give him a chance to clean up before heading across the fence line to meet the neighbors. JD met them at the side gate, opening it with a flourish worthy of an old-time butler.

"Afternoon, Congressman Barlowe," the old wrangler greeted him with an enthusiastic handshake and a sunny smile. "Welcome to Whittaker Ranch."

"Thanks for having me," he replied easily, but Ty caught him flexing his hand a little as they walked toward the house. "Ty tells me your family was one of the original settlers of this area. How long have you been here?"

The simple question kicked off one of JD's favorite subjects, and he launched into the Whittakers' history while the three of them settled on the wide front porch for some fresh cookies and iced tea. Ty caught a glimpse of Jessie in the kitchen, and he tapped on the window. When she looked out, he held up a cookie and gave her an approving thumbs-up. Cheerful as ever, she beamed at him as if he'd just made her entire day.

JD stopped for a sip of tea, and Craig said, "I understand you and your daughter are heading up the Mustang Ridge Conservancy. I'd love to hear what you've got in mind and how I can help. Is there any chance we could all meet while I'm here?"

"Oh, she'll be along," the older man replied in a vague tone that warned Ty something was going on. He'd learned long ago that Morgan Whittaker was the most unpredictable girl on the planet. While her innate spontaneity usually captivated him, in this case, it could prove to be a problem.

Out of the corner of his eye, he picked up some motion inside the barn nearest the house and subtly shifted in his seat for a better look. When he got a glimpse of what she had in mind, he couldn't help grinning at her ingenuity.

Decked out in her best western gear of hand-tooled leather and plenty of shiny accents, Sadie jogged toward the house, leading a flashy bay he'd never seen. Clyde trailed behind the mare like a lovelorn colt, the slack line making it obvious that he was following out of devotion rather than because Morgan was leading him. When the little caravan stopped at the base of the porch steps, Sadie tossed her head in a greeting that jingled with the sound of well-polished silver.

Smiling like a country boy who'd spent too long in the city, Craig got to his feet and went down the steps. Tipping the hat Ty had loaned him, he said, "Morgan Whittaker, I presume."

"I am." Leaning down, she offered a hand

gloved in fawn-colored leather. "Welcome to Mustang Ridge, Congressman Barlowe."

"Craig."

"Nice to meet you, Craig."

They traded a not-very-subtle look of mutual interest, and Ty felt his eyes narrowing all on their own. Not that he cared if Morgan flirted with their visitor, he groused silently. Who she made eyes at was her own business. Besides, she was just doing it to make a good impression on someone who could bring the right kind of attention to her cause. Probably.

Craig stroked Sadie's forehead, even while his eyes were still locked on Morgan. When he finally looked away, he said, "What a beauty."

Whether he was referring to woman or horse, Ty couldn't say. He also didn't know why that mattered to him, but it did. Fortunately, Clyde moved forward to claim his share of the attention, effectively breaking their moment. Smothering a grin, Ty made a mental note to double up on his buddy's grain that night.

"She's half mustang," Morgan explained, her voice ripe with pride. "She was born into the herd that lives on the wild land at the north end of the ranch. Since you're here, I thought you might like to see for yourself what we're fighting so hard to protect."

"I'd love to. And it'd be a lot more fun to ride out there than drive." Clyde bumped his shoulder, and Craig laughed as he reached out to ruffle the chestnut's long forelock. "It's good to see you, too, Clyde. How've you been?"

"Ty told us that you haven't seen each other much lately," Morgan commented. "How is it you remember his horse's name?"

Craig tapped his temple with another grin. "Mind like a steel trap. Just don't ask me what I had for breakfast, 'cause I'd say it was something gray and soupy."

"Bad oatmeal?"

"At three a.m., everything's gray and soupy."

Morgan laughed as if that was the funniest thing she'd ever heard, and Ty clamped his jaw around a disgusted groan. The fact the she and Craig were hitting it off was a good thing, he reminded himself, and this meeting had been his idea, after all. He just hadn't anticipated that they'd get along *this* well.

When he felt someone staring at him, he noticed JD watching him closely, a knowing look on his weathered face. Returning the look with a tight smile, Ty stood and went down to claim Clyde's reins from Morgan.

"If we're riding out to the ridge, we'd best get going. The girls will be home from school soon."

"Jessie's got kid duty today," Morgan informed him. Turning one of her spectacular megawatt smiles on Craig, she added, "I've got all the time in the world."

"That sounded like an invitation to me," the congressman replied, taking the bay's reins from her. "And who is this?"

"Lucy. She's gentle as a lamb, so you should do fine with her."

"Hello, Lucy," he said, rubbing her gleaming neck in the kind of getting-to-know-you gesture that clearly said he knew his way around horses. After a few moments, he swung himself expertly into the saddle and motioned to Morgan. "Lead on, boss."

She loved being called that, Ty thought darkly, hearing her laughter trail behind her as she and Sadie moved off at a smooth jog. Almost immediately, she went into tour guide mode, pointing out the various animals they'd rescued over the years and farther out, the impressive herd of cattle that had been the lifeblood of Whittaker Ranch since the beginning.

And, like an afterthought, Ty hauled himself onto Clyde's back to take up the rear. It

was far from the position he would have preferred, and he nudged his horse into a lope to
catch up with the others. Bookended between
Ty and Morgan, Craig addressed comments
from one to the other with an ease that made
it obvious he had a lot of experience playing
diplomat in just this type of situation.

"So, Ty," he said at one point, "now I see
what you meant about how special this place
is. I've been all over the state, but Mustang
Ridge has a quality all its own. Why do you
think that is?"

"It's far enough off the beaten path that no
one's ever bothered to monkey with it. All
this," he added, motioning to the wide-open
landscape surrounding them, "has been here
forever, but the only folks who know about it
like the place just the way it is."

"That's not entirely true," Craig reminded
him in a serious tone. "I've gotten emails
from people around town who are just as passionate about allowing the development as the
conservancy is about preventing it." Glancing at Morgan, he frowned. "Sorry to be the
bearer of bad news, but I'd imagine you already know that."

"I'd have to be deaf not to," she shot back,
clearly irked by his attempt to soften a blow
she'd already taken. That was Morgan, Ty

mused. Those breezy looks did a great job of masking a backbone that had been forged from pure steel. Now that he was getting to know her again, it occurred to him that he'd actually begun to admire the woman's determination more than her beauty.

Although, quite honestly, both were pretty amazing.

"What are you grinning at over there?" the lady in question demanded, nailing him with a scorching look that could have withered an entire section of hay.

For some reason, her irritation only made him grin more. "Just admiring the day, MJ."

"MJ?" Craig echoed in a curious tone.

"Morgan Jo," she explained, her look sliding into the icy range in a heartbeat. "No one calls me that anymore."

"Except me," Ty continued, unable to resist yanking her chain. "'Cause I'm special."

"Hate to break this to you, cowboy," Craig commented with a chuckle, "but from where I'm sitting, I think you're dead meat."

"Aw, I ain't afraid of her."

"You should be," his friend cautioned, sending their trail ride boss a smile. "Morgan strikes me as the type of woman a smart man doesn't mess with."

"Got that right," she retorted, kicking Sadie

into a lope, as if daring them to keep pace with the half-mustang mare.

"She's incredible," Craig said, admiration lighting his tired eyes. "I can't believe you were stupid enough to break up with her."

He set off to catch up with her, leaving Ty behind with the comment ringing in his ears. "Yeah," he muttered to himself as he spurred Clyde to follow. "Me, neither."

Chapter Five

After their refreshing run, Morgan reined Sadie into a walk, stopping beside a gurgling creek to give the horses a chance to drink. Lucy began browsing the nearby trees for a snack, and Morgan clucked at her in disapproval. "Lucy, you know better than that. Craig, you need to get her head up or she'll munch all day."

"It's not a big deal," he said, reaching down to pat her gleaming neck. "She hasn't even tried to throw me, so I'd say she's earned a treat for being so nice to the city slicker."

Morgan shrugged, figuring there was no harm in it, and if the mare's habit didn't bother him, then she wasn't going to press the issue. When she noticed Ty staring off into the distance, she twisted in her saddle to follow his line of sight and frowned when she noticed a chromed-out 4x4 parked in a stand of trees.

"Who's that?" she asked.

"No idea. One of the neighbors get a new car?"

She snorted at the suggestion. "Folks around here don't have money for a flashy car like that."

"I was thinking the same thing," Ty said absently, his eyes meeting hers in a somber look. "I was also thinking he's set himself up on that public land you've been using for your wild ponies."

"He could be from Cartwright Energy," Craig suggested. "Surveying, maybe."

Morgan was impressed that someone as busy as him could recall the name of a single development firm from among the dozens of petitions he must receive every week. Unfortunately, his curious tone didn't sit right with her, and she glared at him. "You make it sound like it's not something we should be worried about."

"Surveying public land isn't a crime," he reminded her in a calm, legalistic manner that made her want to scream. "I don't see any excavating or drilling equipment around, so if he's just taking measurements or collecting surface samples, there's not a problem."

"For you, maybe," Morgan spat, quickly losing patience with her handsome guest. "I have a big problem with it. That's how these things start, looking all innocent and aboveboard. Then, before the locals know it, they're living in the middle of a deconstruction zone."

"Give 'em an inch, they take a mile," Ty agreed, frowning in disapproval. "You know how businesses like these work, Craig. You must've seen every trick in the book by now."

"Not every one, but enough to know you've both got a point."

"That's enough nonsense," Morgan announced, lifting Sadie's head and pointing her nose in the right direction. "Let's go have a little chat with our visitor."

Craig responded with a shake of his head. "Sorry, but I'll have to beg off on that one. I might be dealing with this guy later, and it wouldn't be good for me to give anyone the impression that I'm taking sides."

Seriously? Morgan wanted to ask, then thought better of it. He was the politician, not her, and she had no idea how Washington worked. She had to trust that Craig knew what he was doing and that him staying out of this particular fray would prove to be beneficial to their cause later on. Turning to Ty, she gave him the I-dare-you look that had worked on him since they were kids. "How 'bout you?"

That earned her one of his wide-open country boy grins. "I wouldn't miss it."

Possibly not the smartest approach, she acknowledged as they moved toward the intruder, but she had to give him credit for stepping up. He hadn't hesitated even the tiniest bit when she all but challenged him to come along. Dad would groan that they were both crazy, but at least it was the same brand of crazy. In spite of their rocky personal history, it was comforting to know that Ty wasn't going to just stand by and let her confront this unwelcome stranger on her own.

Not that it mattered all that much, she amended grimly. She would've done it one way or the other.

As she and Ty approached their squatting visitor, he glanced up from his tablet with an annoyed expression. By the time they reined the horses to stand, he'd closed down whatever he was working on and stood up tall. "May I help you?"

"I was going to ask you the same thing," Morgan replied in the fake-polite tone she used on phone solicitors.

"I'm fine. Thanks."

Well, that wasn't helpful, she groused silently as he turned his back and strode away. So much for manners, she decided, spurring Sadie into a jog that easily overtook him. Careful to avoid crowding him, the horse stopped and spun, facing him head-on in the cutting horse stance that came naturally to her. Sadie had never tipped a barrel or lost the attention of any calf she'd ever faced, and this greenhorn was no match for her.

The man's irritated look was back, but it quickly faded when Clyde came up on his other side, effectively cutting him off from his fancy rental SUV. Ty caught her eye and gave her a slight nod, as if to say that whatever happened next was totally up to her.

And Morgan wasn't too proud to admit— at least to herself—that she liked it.

Swinging down from the saddle, she strolled up to the stranger and decided on a softer approach. She took off one of her gloves and extended her hand. "I think we got off on the wrong foot here. I'm Morgan Whittaker."

"I know perfectly well who you are," he informed her testily. His tone got Sadie's attention, and she took a single step closer, pressing up against Morgan's shoulder in a protective gesture so typical of the intelligent creatures Morgan was fighting to save. The man's expression softened a bit, and his face cracked into something akin to a smile. "You have a beautiful horse."

Morgan knew she couldn't really take credit for that. The gorgeous palomino was God's handiwork, but she appreciated the effort he'd made and forced a smile. "Thank you, Mr.—?"

"Nelson. Bill Nelson." This time, he took her hand for a tentative shake. "I'm an assayer for Cartwright Energy. But I'm guessing you already knew that."

"Not the specifics, but I figured you were associated with them. This spread—" she indicated the expansive property they were standing in the middle of "—is pretty close to my family's ranch. I thought Cartwright was interested in the Bridger Mountain slopes farther up. What are you doing this far south?"

"Covering all the bases," he replied cryptically, obviously making an attempt to keep his mission as vague as possible.

He wasn't exactly trespassing, but having anyone this close to her beloved mustangs made her uneasy, to say the least. While Morgan was hunting for a way to extend their conversation and find out a bit more about his purpose, Ty swung down to stand beside her.

When Bill got a closer look at the former bull rider, his eyes nearly bugged out of his head.

"You're Ty Wilkins."

"Last time I checked," Ty joked, offering one of his scarred hands with a disarming grin that still seemed to fool everyone but Morgan.

"I'm a huge rodeo fan, and I've seen you compete at least a dozen times," Bill gushed in an excited voice. "My friends and I were convinced you must've been superglued to those bulls."

"Not quite, but thanks."

"What are you doing here? I mean, not that it's any of my business, but I haven't seen you on the circuit this year. You're not thinking of retiring, are you?"

A twinge of sorrow clouded those hazel eyes, but it quickly vanished behind the friendly twinkle that normally warmed the gold accents. "Not sure yet. For now, I'm working with Morgan and the Mustang Ridge Conservancy. Since we're against the prospecting your company is suggesting, you can see why we'd be interested in what you're doing out here."

"I can," Bill conceded with a frown. "But I'm not allowed to discuss my assignment with anyone other than my boss. I'm sure you understand."

Ty cocked his head in a display of thinking that one over, and Morgan had to swallow a laugh. He might drive her completely bonkers on a regular basis, but she had to admit that he had a real knack for dealing with people.

"Not really," the tall cowboy finally said, adding yet another lazy grin. "But I'm a quick study. Why don't you explain it to me?"

Bill hesitated, and Morgan couldn't believe that he might actually disregard his orders and confide in Ty. Then the professional shutters came down, and he slowly shook his head. "I can't do that. I'm aware of the property lines that are in place out here, and I'll stay well clear of the Whittaker boundaries," he added, aiming the comment Morgan's way. "That's all I'm legally required to do."

His reference to the law got Morgan's back up. Unfortunately for him, it also got her mind spinning in a different direction. "Who gave Cartwright the idea to come digging out here in the first place?"

"I wouldn't know that."

"But even if you did," she pressed in growing dislike of his I'm-just-following-orders attitude, "you wouldn't tell us. Right?"

Bill gave Ty an unmistakable guy's look. "Let me guess. She's the brains?"

Ty gave a single nod, leaving his head at an angle that left the brim of his hat shading his eyes. The stance reminded her of a lone-wolf character in an old Western, and she had to fight off a grin. He really was good at this.

"Look," Bill went on, including both of them in an apologetic glance. "I've heard a little about what's going on here, and I can honestly say I sympathize with your position. But I have a family to support, and as a geologist, this is the best position I've ever had. No matter what my personal opinion on this issue might be, I can't do anything that might get me fired."

"That I understand," Ty commented, adding a heavy sigh. "We've all got a job to do, right?"

"Right."

Recognizing that even Ty's considerable personal charms weren't going to get them anywhere this time, Morgan conceded defeat. At least for now. "Well, I have a family legacy to protect, not to mention the environment that your company seems to have so little respect for. If you ever decide to switch sides, let me know. We could use a good geologist in our corner."

She'd learned never to leave the house without a few business cards, and she slid one from the rear pocket of her jeans and handed it to him. Then, because there was nothing more to say, she turned and walked back to where Sadie was quietly grazing within sight of the herd that her mother had been part of years ago.

The two men had a quick exchange, and then Ty fell in beside her again as they rode back toward where they'd left their guest. Even from a distance, she could see that Craig was lounging in the shade of a gnarled elm, thumbing through screens on his phone, while Lucy munched on daisies.

"What did Bill say to you?" Morgan asked without thinking. It was really none of her business, but she had to admit that Ty's ease with people both frustrated and fascinated her. She didn't share that particular talent, and she couldn't help wondering how it worked.

To her aggravation, Ty chuckled. "He was impressed that even out in the middle of nowhere, you had a business card."

The comment only irked her more. "What? He thinks I'm an empty-headed blonde who doesn't know how to run a nonprofit organization?"

"Well, now, he didn't exactly say it like

that," Ty drawled, sending her one of those infernal grins.

"But he was thinking it, I'm sure." Blowing out an exasperated breath, she went on seething. "How come folks have such a hard time viewing me seriously, but they immediately take to the rodeo star?"

Ty's grin evaporated, and he glanced down at his hands, fiddling with Clyde's reins in a rare show of discomfort. When he lifted his gaze to hers, the lighthearted twinkle was gone. "Got me. But I'd imagine it won't be too long before I find out how people are gonna react to plain old Ty Wilkins."

Morgan hadn't considered how difficult that transition might be for him. Always at home in the spotlight, being a regular person was a real comedown for him. And, because she appreciated him backing her up with Bill Nelson, she decided to be nice.

"There's nothing plain or old about you, cowboy," she said, astonished by how easily the compliment rolled off her tongue. "Folks around here like you because of who you are, not what kind of trophies you've won."

That seemed to lift his spirits, and he gave her a grateful smile. "Then I guess it's a good thing I decided to come home."

Morgan found herself smiling back at him.

"I can't believe I'm saying this, but I agree with you."

For some reason, he pulled out his phone and aimed the camera in her direction. "Would you mind repeating that? No one's gonna believe it unless I have a video."

In response, Morgan stuck her tongue out at him and spurred Sadie into a lope that left him eating her dust. That was where he belonged, in the past that she'd been trying to put behind her for so long. But somehow, he'd popped up in her life again, and sooner or later she'd have to figure out what that meant.

But that would have to wait. Right now, she had a congressman to dazzle.

"So, Craig," Jessie said while passing the mashed potatoes, "what do you like best about Washington?"

After chewing thoughtfully for a few moments, he swallowed and replied, "The weather."

JD sat back and chuckled. "An honest politician? I didn't think they made those anymore."

"There's a few of us left," Craig assured him with an easygoing grin. "More than you might assume, based on the news that comes out of the Beltway. Lots of us are there to represent the interests of the folks who elected us, and we do our best for them every day. It's not easy, but when you get it right, there's no better feeling."

This was what he'd liked about the young congressman when they first met at one of his campaign events a few years ago, Ty recalled fondly. Not many politicians treated voters to barbecue and corn bread under a tent at a rodeo. Actually, he couldn't think of another one, and that made Craig's down-to-earth approach stand out all the more.

"Do you think you can help us fight Cartwright?" Morgan asked in her usual direct way. Ty much preferred it to her flirting with the guy, but the relief he felt seemed out of proportion to the situation. Shoving that thought aside, he waited to hear what their potential champion had to say.

"Managing the local issues will be up to you," he responded in an overly careful tone that clearly riled his hostess.

"Meaning there's nothing you can do," she retorted in an accusing tone. When her scathing glare moved from Craig to land on Ty, he fought the urge to squirm.

"I didn't say that," Craig reminded her patiently, pulling her attention back to him. Ty was insanely grateful for the reprieve, and he sent his friend a thankful look.

"Then what are you saying?" JD growled, scowling like a grizzly who'd been awakened a month too early. "'Cause what I'm hearing is some fancy lawyer's double-talk."

Craig met that with a half smile. "It's true that I'm a lawyer by trade, but I'm hardly a fancy one. What I meant is that I'll do what I can in DC, but I can't handle the job all on my own. The efforts of you and the others involved in the conservancy will be crucial to whether or not Mustang Ridge succeeds where so many other resource-rich areas have failed."

Ty caught a whiff of what he was trying not to say and filled in the blank. "You're talking about the locals who don't support the development, right?"

"In part. From what you and Morgan have told me, the town's split pretty much down the middle on this issue. Development brings jobs and money into an area, and that's tempting for a lot of residents."

"But even if they find what they're looking for, when the resource they were after is gone, what then?" Morgan asked, skepticism sparking in her eyes. "Cartwright will head off to their next project, and we'll be left with a huge mess and no way to clean it up."

She'd always been smart as a whip, able to look beyond the obvious to whatever was lurking beneath the surface. Ty had no trouble imagining her starting this fight on her own, gradually pulling in others who shared her feelings but weren't aware of the dangers the energy company's exploration posed.

Craig slid him a bemused look. "Forget about you coming to DC to talk to the Natural Resources Committee. We should bring Morgan in to tell them all what-for. No one in their right mind could ignore all that passion."

Morgan's eyes dropped on Ty like a hawk, and again he fought the urge to squirm. "You're going to testify in front of Congress?"

"We talked about it," he hedged, silently chiding his friend for selling him out this way. "Nothing's been decided, though."

Fortunately, Craig jumped in to help. "It was my idea. I thought Ty's name recognition might help your cause. Sometimes when ordinary folks come in, they get a little tongue-tied and—"

The Whittakers all burst out laughing, and Ty had to grin. Leaning toward their guest, he murmured, "Not a problem for Morgan."

Craig took the ribbing in stride and held up

his hands in surrender. "Okay, you got me. But here's an idea." Pausing, he glanced from Morgan at the foot of the table to Ty. "Why don't you both come as my guests? That gets you double the exposure, and it just might make the difference between your petition receiving immediate attention and getting set on the pile for later review."

"We don't have time for 'later review,'" Morgan pointed out, air-quoting the last two words with a derisive expression. "According to Bill Nelson, Cartwright's planning to bring in their drilling equipment within a couple months."

"So much for community involvement," Ryan grumbled. "That meeting was nothing but a sham to make folks think they had a say in what'd be happening here."

"At work, I heard the company just leased an office in our building," Jessie chimed in. "I asked the main lobby receptionist about it, and she heard they signed up for three years."

Ben scowled at that. "That means they're planning on sticking around at least that long."

"Even if they don't, that expense is just chicken feed to a big firm like that," Morgan added in disgust. "And if they find what they're looking for, they'll be around even longer."

"Business owners would like that, even if

the ranchers don't," Ty commented, beginning to see the dilemma his quaint hometown was facing.

"That's the problem," Morgan acknowledged, glancing into the living room, where Allie and Hannah were stretched out on a braided rug building a log cabin village. "If we let them in and then change our minds about what they're doing, there's no telling how long it might take to get rid of them."

"Legally, it's almost impossible," Craig confirmed in a somber voice. "Once the land is sold and the leases and land-use documents have been signed, you'll have no legal recourse to stop the activity. Your best chance is to prevent the exploration altogether. I've seen cases where a company doesn't find what they anticipated but stumbled on some other resource and mined that instead to minimize their losses."

After some more grim back-and-forth, JD put an end to the conversation by sliding his chair back and standing. "That's enough doom and gloom for me. I'm going for a ride."

"I hope I'm not the reason you're leaving your own table," Craig said apologetically as he stood.

"Not a bit. We need to know what we're up against, and thanks to you, we've got a much better idea of how tough this fight is gonna be." The weathered rancher extended his hand with a smile. "But that won't scare us off, so don't you worry."

"That's good to know." After JD had left, the young politician remained standing. "I've got a few dozen emails to get through, so I'll call it a night. Thanks so much for the home cooking and the great company. Nights like this remind me of why I do what I do," he added, sending a smile Morgan's way.

She returned it, all memory of their earlier spat apparently gone. "I'll walk you and Ty out."

Feeling like a tagalong little brother, Ty wished everyone a good night and followed them to the front door. After they said their goodbyes, he and Craig strolled toward the common fence line and stepped through to the Wilkins side.

"So," Craig began in a casual tone that made Ty suspicious for some reason. "You really have to tell me—why did you break up with that incredible woman in there?"

"We were together awhile. It didn't work out, but we're still friends." At least, he hoped they were. He had to admit that even for him, sometimes it was hard to tell.

"She's an amazing woman, and she strikes me as the type who could cut a guy off at the knees anytime she wanted. I pity anyone foolish enough to go up against her on something that's really important to her."

"Like saving Mustang Ridge?" When Craig nodded, Ty stopped and turned to face him. "Be straight with me, Craig. Do we have a chance?"

After considering that for a few moments, he nodded. "Yes, but you have to get it right the first time. There will be a hundred other petitions just like yours, just as important, and just as prickly for the committee to deal with. This country needs to find and develop its own resources so we don't have to import as much as we're currently doing. That brings oil and fuel prices down, and that benefits everyone from young families to senior citizens living on fixed incomes."

"Okay, I get that. Now that you've heard our plans, what do you need from me?"

"I really think you and Morgan would make a great one-two punch in front of the committee." After a long pause, he went on. "I'm happy to sponsor you and make the introductions, but I think it's best if I stay out of the process for the most part."

"Why?"

Craig gave him a knowing look that made Ty feel transparent. "I saw how you reacted whenever I talked to Morgan. It's pretty obvious there's something going on there, and I'm not willing to lose a friend over a woman. Not even one as incredible as her."

"You're crazy," Ty chided with a laugh. "I told you, she and I are just friends."

"I heard you. I just don't believe you."

Craig began walking again, leaving Ty standing in the middle of the pasture staring after him. Clyde was grazing nearby, and when he noticed Ty was alone, he came ambling over to sniff his pockets in search of a treat.

"Nothing tonight, buddy," he said, offering a quick jaw scratch instead. The powerful gelding accepted that gladly enough, then head-butted him so hard, Ty nearly fell down. Regaining his balance, he laughed. "All right, you win. Let's go."

As they made their way toward the barn, he puzzled over Craig's errant comments about Morgan. For all his instincts about people, it was weird that the congressman would so completely miss the mark when it came to something like that.

Oh, well, Ty thought with a mental shrug. Even a sharp-minded lawyer could be wrong once in a while.

Chapter Six

One afternoon, Ty was in his side pasture re-
placing a cracked fence post when he heard a
child's voice call out, "Mr. Wilkins!"

Looking up, he found Hannah waving at
him. She and Allie were sitting on a woven
blanket under a tall elm in the Whittakers'
front yard, with Morgan's faithful Aussie
shepherd, Skye, keeping watch over them.

Waving, he hollered back, "Hello to you,
too. What're you ladies up to?"

"Having a tea party," she explained, lifting
an old-fashioned china cup and saucer for him
to see. "Would you like to come?"

Ty's heart jumped at the invitation, and he
took a moment to let it settle back down before he did something stupid. The girl had
no idea who he was, he reminded himself
sternly. To her, he was just a neighbor who

happened to be within earshot. Still, the unexpected invitation to spend some time with
his daughters gave him a warm, satisfied feeling he'd seldom experienced.

"I'd love to," he finally replied, dusting
his hands off on his jeans before stepping
through the fence. "But only if you call me
Ty like everyone else does."

"But you're a grown-up," Hannah protested, a frown creasing her freckled cheeks.
"We're supposed to call grown-ups mister or
missus."

One of Morgan's rules, he assumed with a
chuckle. After sitting cross-legged on an un-
occupied piece of blanket, he glanced around
and then leaned in. "Can you two keep a secret?"

Hannah nodded immediately, eyes shining
at the idea of being in on something no one
else knew. Allie took a few beats longer, but
she did the same, adding a curious look that
he took to mean she was interested in hearing what he had to say.

"Okay, here it is." Lowering his voice, he
went on. "I'm not grown-up all the way."

"You're tall," Allie commented in a serious
voice that told him she'd taken him literally.
Over the past few days, he'd done some research on autism, and he'd learned that was

a feature of the condition. It came in a distant second to the fact that she'd responded to him directly for the first time, and without her usual hesitation. Knowing that he'd forged a connection with the reserved child— however slight—made him feel like he'd just scored a touchdown.

"Uncle Ryan and Uncle Ben are tall," Hannah added while she poured something from her teapot into a mug imprinted with the Whittaker Ranch logo, which was a horse running past the outline of a mountain range. Handing it to him, she added, "But you're even bigger than them."

"And proud of it," Ty said, saluting her with the cup before taking a cautious sip. When he discovered it was nothing but water and a dash of sugar, he finished it off in a single gulp before holding out his empty mug. "That's the best tea I've ever had. Could I get a refill?"

She obliged him and then set the pot down in the center of the blanket. A partially eaten plate of cookies was there, too, and he noticed Skye staring at the treats intently. When she sent him a hopeful look, he snagged one and broke it neatly, tossing half to her before popping the rest in his mouth. "These are delicious. Did you girls make them?"

"Mommy did," Allie told him shyly.

"You're kidding." She shook her head, and the unease that darkened her features made him want to kick himself. Very quickly, he said, "I believe you, honey. It's just that I didn't know your mom liked to bake."

"Mommy says whatever we do together is fun for her," Hannah informed him sweetly. A gust of wind blew through the yard, toppling one of the dolls that had come in for the party. She reached over to set the toy upright and patted her bonneted head in a maternal way she must have learned from Morgan. "There you go, Chantilly. Would you like some more tea?"

While she filled the doll's cup, Ty looked around at his fellow partygoers. He counted a dozen dolls, four teddy bears and a stuffed something or other that was so ratty he couldn't begin to identify it. Hoping to get an answer without sounding like a clueless adult, he said, "I haven't met everyone here yet. Can you introduce us?"

"Sure," Hannah replied, listing their names in a rapid-fire manner that she'd clearly inherited from her mother. The bedraggled member of the group was named Freddie, which didn't help much in the classifying department. So, Ty swallowed his cowboy pride and asked what kind of animal he was.

"A koala," Allie answered, stroking his furry head gently. "He's from Australia."

"Allie knows a lot about animals," Hannah added proudly, smiling over at her twin. "When we read books about them, she remembers way more about them than I do."

What a great kid, Ty thought. Whatever challenges Morgan had faced while she'd been raising them, she'd done an incredible job. He only wished he'd been part of the picture from the start. While his daughters traded girlie small talk, he stretched out on the grass and drank it all in, mulling over what had gone on before he knew they existed.

He'd missed so much, he acknowledged with a heavy heart. Their first smiles, crawling, walking, all those baby memories that his friends with children treasured and shared with him through one social app or another.

And then, he came to one that wasn't so cheerful: the day they discovered that Allie had autism.

He couldn't imagine how that had been for Morgan, to learn that her precious child would need so much extra care, special classes, endless patience. The cowgirl he remembered with equal parts fondness and exasperation had never been the easygoing type, but clearly time and necessity had mellowed that part of her.

At least where her kids were concerned, he recognized, grinning when he recalled the run-ins they'd had in the weeks since he'd come back to town. Around him, Morgan felt confident enough to be her old feisty self. Oddly enough, he didn't mind her prickly nature all that much. So much had changed in his life recently that it was comforting to know there were still some things that had remained the same.

"Hey, guys."

When he heard Morgan's voice, Ty glanced over his shoulder to find her strolling up behind him. Her tone had sounded casual enough, but the set of her delicate jaw warned him that the temperamental cowgirl he remembered so fondly was very much alive and well. Hoping to defuse whatever had her riled up, he lifted his hand in greeting. "Hey yourself. Want some tea?"

The muscles in her cheek relaxed just a bit, but it couldn't disguise the fury sparking in her eyes. Still, she managed to keep her cool as she sat down on the blanket opposite him. "Sure, thanks."

While Hannah poured her a cup and Allie handed her a cookie, Ty was struck by the fact that a first-time visitor to the Whittaker Ranch would assume they were a nice, happy family taking time out in the middle of a warm afternoon for some snacks and lukewarm water in fancy teacups. If he hadn't been so stupid all those years ago, this kind of scene could have been his reality instead of something he'd just stumbled upon by sheer good fortune.

But thanks to his stubborn pride, all he could do was wish for more.

"How's it going out there?" Ty asked.

His lame attempt at conversation got him a scathing look. "We lost three calves to wolves last night, and there's a section of fence down on the pasture we were planning to move some cattle into today. You?"

"Pulling rotted posts so I can replace them," he replied, grateful to have something concrete to tell her. Spending his days cleaning and lounging had gotten old, and he felt better now that he was actually accomplishing something. Beneath the brim of her straw cowgirl hat, he saw the worried shadows around her eyes. Instinct told him that something beyond ranch concerns was bothering her, but he couldn't begin to determine what it might be. She had so much on her plate, it could've been any one of a dozen things.

Then he heard the front door creak open and glanced over to see JD coming onto the porch, a glass of iced tea in his hand. He sank into one of the redwood rocking chairs with a tired sigh, leaning his head against the high back and closing his eyes. He sat there like that, holding the glass but not drinking anything, for so long that Ty started to wonder if he'd fallen asleep that way. Finally, he took a sip and set the glass down, linking his hands together on his chest before going back to his power-napping pose.

Slanting a look at Morgan, Ty realized she'd been closely watching her father since he'd emerged from the house. The worried expression she wore answered Ty's question about what had been troubling her, and he hunted for a way to ease her mind without setting off her flash-fire temper.

"I've got Clyde corralled on the other side of the barn, so he's not going anywhere," he said. "That means what I'm working on can wait. Would you like another set of hands out there?"

"Ryan and I can handle it."

No mention of JD, he noticed. He wondered how she was planning to convince her father not to head back out when there was still work to be done. Hoping he'd read the situation correctly, Ty pressed a little. "It's pretty hot today, and JD looks wiped out. I'd be happy to fill in for him so he can take the afternoon off."

Morgan's sharp gaze softened a bit, and this time he got an actual smile out of her. "It's nice of you to offer. I've been trying to figure out how to tell him he needs to call it a day. He's not an invalid, but he's not the bull he used to be, either. Don't you dare tell him I said that," she warned, pointing a stern finger at him for emphasis. "He'd be furious to find out I think he's anything less than Superman."

"Not a chance," Ty replied with a grin. "I'd prefer to keep my head attached to my shoulders."

She laughed at that, and joining in was the easiest thing he'd done in a long time.

Hannah gave her mother a confused look. "I don't get it. Everyone's head is attached."

"Ty means that Grandpa would take his head off if he suggested Grandpa needed some help," Morgan explained with a smile. "Not really, though. It's an expression that means the person would get really mad at you."

"That's bad," Allie commented quietly.

"It can be," Ty allowed, directing his comment at the shy child. "But sometimes if you want to help someone, you have to risk making them angry."

"Why?" she asked, clearly baffled.

"Because it's better for them. Sometimes folks—especially stubborn ones like your grandpa—keep going the way they are even when they shouldn't."

"You know all about that, don't you?" Morgan asked. While it was clearly a challenge, her voice was calm now, and the anger had left her eyes. Ty wasn't sure what she was trying to do, but he took her calmer demeanor as a good sign.

"Yeah, I do. My grandfather used to tell us that pride is a good servant but a terrible master." He got two very blank looks and realized he needed to explain. "It means that being proud is good to a point, but sometimes it can get outta control. When it does, you're in trouble."

"Did you get in trouble?" Hannah asked, eyes widening at the idea.

"Yeah, I did. And someone I really loved got hurt because of it. I'll always regret that."

"You should apologize," his sweet daughter informed him in a very grown-up voice.

"That way, they'll know you feel bad about what you did. Right, Mommy?"

"True," Morgan agreed. Then, to his astonishment, she added an understanding look. "But I'm sure Ty has done that already. Sometimes it just takes a while for the other person to forgive you for what happened."

After that, their conversation swung to what was going on at school, and what their friends were going to do on their upcoming summer vacations. While Ty followed along and made appropriate comments here and there, part of his mind was focused on the bone Morgan had so unexpectedly tossed him.

Was it possible that she'd begun to forgive him for abandoning her seven years ago? And if she had, was it possible that sometime in the future they'd be able to find a way to be a family? Granted, it wouldn't be the traditional kind, where they got married and then had a bunch of kids. But given some effort and persistence, he thought maybe they could be friends and work together to raise their daughters.

Right now, from where he was sitting, that looked pretty good.

"Ty, I gotta admit something to you," Ryan began, leaning on a newly set fence post in the

Whittakers' expansive back pasture. When the former bull rider looked over, her younger brother grinned and shook his head. "You're a better ranch hand than I figured you'd be. When Morgan texted me that you offered to help, I figured you'd make it twenty minutes and then we'd be carting you back to your place in a heap."

"Hard work's good for the soul," Ty replied, adding the kind of sheepish grin Morgan couldn't recall ever seeing on him before his stunning downfall. "I always assumed that was one of Grandpa's clichés, but it turns out he was right. As a bonus, on a hot day like this, you even drop a few pounds you don't need to be carrying around."

His easygoing attitude was typical Ty, Morgan knew, but there was a slight tension in his jaw that told her he was putting up a good front for their sakes. The severe back injury he'd suffered wasn't something that healed and disappeared. It was the sort of thing that dogged you for the rest of your life and had to be managed carefully to keep you out of a wheelchair.

While she recognized that he was a grown man who was perfectly capable of taking care of himself, she couldn't help worrying that in his eagerness to be helpful, he'd overdone it. And that he'd regret his generosity when he tried to drag himself out of bed tomorrow morning. His mention of the heat was her opportunity to let him off the hook, and just as she'd done while learning to cut calves from a herd, she dove into the opening.

"We're almost out of water, so I'll drive back and pick up some cold gallons from the house. Could you give me a hand, Ty?"

She half expected a protest from her brother, but Ryan caught her eye and gave her a slight nod. So, he'd noticed Ty laboring, too, she thought as she sent back a quick smile. Two years younger than her, Ryan could be a real pain, but he also had a big, generous heart. Like her, he wasn't one to watch someone suffer quietly without at least trying to do something about it.

"If you're worried about me, I'm fine," Ty objected stubbornly. "If I stay here, Ryan and I can set a couple more posts before you get back."

"Not a chance," Ryan retorted, stabbing the handheld posthole digger into a pile of loose soil. "I'm past being ready for a break."

Striding past them both, he sprawled out underneath a slender oak whose shade was just wide enough to cover his lanky frame. Sliding his sweat-soaked cowboy hat forward, he crossed his arms over his chest in an obvious message to anyone passing by that if they disturbed him, they'd quickly be wishing they hadn't.

Ty stared at him for a few moments before shrugging. "Whatever. Let's go."

Pleased to get even a grudging concession from the most intractable man on the planet, Morgan was feeling pretty proud of herself as she walked over to the beat-up ranch truck and climbed into the cab. Her buoyant attitude was short-lived, evaporating as she watched Ty laboriously haul himself into the passenger seat. He stared out the open window in a blatant attempt to avoid having a conversation with her, and she decided it was best to leave him alone as she started the engine.

"My back's gonna be fine, y'know," he said, still not looking at her.

Morgan was torn between humoring him and being direct. Coddling people wasn't her style, even her girls, and she finally decided to heed her instincts. "Sure it will, but you're not there yet. Until you are, you have to be smart about how much you do. You don't want to push so hard that you set yourself back to where you were a few months ago."

That got her a groan from her difficult passenger. "All that physical therapy. Some days, I honestly thought I was gonna lose my mind."

"Apparently, they did a good job, because you're in better shape than I thought you'd be."

Horrified that she'd basically just confessed that she'd been following his heartrending story in the news, she clamped her runaway mouth shut and prayed that he was too preoccupied with his discomfort to notice her slip.

He wasn't.

Turning slightly to face her, he winced but managed a version of his old cocky grin. "You were keeping tabs on me?"

"Not exactly. I mean, everyone in town was talking about what happened to you at that competition, and there was no way to ignore it completely."

The grin shifted into a knowing look, accompanied by a bemused twinkle of gold in his eyes. "Which you know, because you tried."

"Yeah," she conceded with a sigh. Glancing over, she went on. "I'm really glad you're doing better, Ty. In spite of what happened with us, I never wished you any harm."

"I'm not sure I deserved that kind of grace from you, but thanks."

So close on the heels of the humor, the remorse in his voice made her heart twist in sympathy. She'd made enough mistakes in her life to know that forgiving yourself was the only way to put them in the past where they belonged. But when you hurt someone as deeply as Ty had done to her, your own attitude was only part of the equation.

Pulling off to the side of the field road, she put the truck in Park and swiveled to face him squarely. Meeting his confused gaze, she quickly ran over their shared past in her mind—good and bad—and came to the conclusion that it was time. Resting a hand on his shoulder, she took a deep breath and forged ahead. "You need to let this go. It's in the past, and that's where it needs to stay."

"You're right, but it's not easy. You know what I mean."

"Yes, but I also know that's the only way you can get over it. We all make mistakes."

After a hesitant look, very quietly he said, "Does that mean you forgive me?"

She thought that one over, even considered telling him she had just to put the matter to rest, but she was a straightforward person by nature. Beyond that, he knew her well enough that if she lied to him, he'd pick up on it in a heartbeat. "No, but I don't think it's impossible. Before we connected again, I couldn't imagine it ever happening."

Relief flooded his rugged features, and the warmth in his gaze made her feel more confident about her decision to confront him and lay everything on the table. "This doesn't seem like enough, but thank you. You don't know how much that means to me."

Actually, she had a pretty good idea, she mused as she made another bold choice that was for this man's own stupid, stubborn good. When she looped around and headed for his place, his gratitude morphed into anger.

"Just turn this thing around, MJ. Heat or no, I'm not quitting in the middle of the afternoon."

"Yes, you are, because I'm not hauling your sorry hide into the hospital tonight when you finally come to your senses and realize you overdid it."

"That's not gonna happen." When she shot him a *really?* look, he gave in with a noise somewhere between a growl and a groan. "Okay, it might happen, but if it does, I'll deal with it then."

"Or you could avoid the problem altogether by being smart. We all have our limitations, cowboy. Even you."

After several seconds, he let out an exasperated breath. "Yeah, I guess you're right. Wish you weren't, though."

"I know," she commented, feeling genuine compassion for him. He was just shy of thirty, and had always been so strong, it must be killing him to be forced to concede that he couldn't do things the rest of them took for granted. Come to think of it, he reminded her of her father, who had trouble admitting — mostly to himself—that he wasn't as spry as he used to be.

Thoughts of Dad gave her an idea, and as she pulled in to park beside Ty's ranch house, she said, "If you want to be useful without killing yourself, you could give Dad a hand with all that paperwork we need to file for the injunction against Cartwright Energy. Stuff like that drives him nuts, and I'd imagine he'd be thrilled to have your help and your company."

"I figured you'd be doing that."

The suggestion made her laugh. "Sure, in all my spare time. Once the girls are on summer vacation, I'll have even less than I do now. I was beginning to wonder how I'd ever get it all done, so Dad volunteered."

"And now he's regretting it," Ty guessed, chuckling. "You're positive he won't mind me stepping in like that? I know how he feels about handling things himself."

"He doesn't seem to mind so much when you're involved. After all, he let you take his place on the fence crew today," she replied, still a little bewildered at how easily he'd stepped aside. Then there was his ongoing fondness for Ty, even though he'd known all along that the absent cowboy was the father of her twins. Morgan still wasn't certain why her dad thought so highly of Ty, but there was no point in denying that he did. She didn't have to understand the reasons to take advantage of the opportunity.

"All right, then, I'll do it. But I want to do some of the physical stuff, too. Not just 'cause you can use me out there, but 'cause it's good for me. I slogged through enough indoor rehab to know the outdoor kind is better. I like being out in the sunshine and fresh air, working with my hands, getting something practical finished. When I'm done, I like looking around and knowing that what I did that day mattered."

"More than trophies and blue ribbons, you mean?"

"Something like that." Staring out the windshield, his face took on a pensive expression. "It's time for me to grow up. I'm not entirely sure how to make that happen, but I'll figure it out."

They'd never had a conversation even remotely like this one, and she was at a loss for what to say. Then inspiration struck, and she quietly said, "I know you will."

Those warm hazel eyes locked with hers, and he gave her another one of his sheepish grins. "Thanks, MJ. Coming from you, that means a lot."

As they got out of the truck and slowly walked inside together, it struck her that for once, she didn't mind him using her old nickname. She wasn't sure what that meant, but it was an undeniable change in her attitude about him. Whether that was good or bad, she couldn't say. But, considering their tumultuous history, finding out which it was should be interesting.

When she got a look at Ty's living room, she stopped dead in her tracks. "Where is everything?"

He glanced around as if he'd forgotten how empty the place was, then said, "Well, the mice got to all the upholstered stuff, and I had to get rid of it. It made for a nice bonfire."

His chuckle sounded forced to her, and the sympathy she'd been feeling for him ratcheted up a notch. But he seemed to be determined to make the best of his bare-bones existence, so she decided it was wise to play along. "At least you don't have to worry about your furniture clashing with the drapes."

His muted grin told her that he appreciated her attempt at humor. The ranch house had three bedrooms off the main living area, and a dated galley kitchen that she could glimpse through the pass-through. "You know, if you tore down that wall, this would be a nice great room to hang out in. Put in an island and some tall stools, a jumbo flat-screen over there—" she pointed "—and you'd have a fabulous spot for entertaining."

"Sounds good. Oh, wait," he added, snapping his fingers. "I'm broke. Guess I'll have to put all that on hold for a while."

"Ryan and Ben did our kitchen reno a couple years ago. It didn't cost that much, and it works a lot better for the family now."

Ty shook his head at the suggestion. "Do I look like Mr. DIY to you?"

Actually, now that she considered his appearance, he still looked like the self-assured cowboy he'd been in high school. Only now, he struck her as being out of place, even in the house that he'd always referred to as home. That seemed odd to her, since he'd grown up here, racing through the living room to the kitchen after school. Getting scolded for leaving his barn boots on and tracking the mess across his mother's immaculate floors.

In her memory, Morgan could still see the two of them sitting on the hearth in the wintertime, sharing a plate of fresh cookies while they thawed out after a ride. The image was so vivid, it almost scared her. Seeking a firmer hold on reality, she reminded herself that the boy in her Norman Rockwell vision had grown into the man who broke her heart and strolled out of her life just when she needed him the most.

The problem was, this time it didn't work. Because the man standing in front of her was in more pain than he'd ever confess, possibly even to himself. And it wasn't just that his back hurt, she knew. His life had imploded, and he had no idea how to go on as anyone other than Ty Wilkins, rodeo champion.

With that morose thought tumbling around in her head, she realized that the silence between them had stretched to an uncomfortable length. To cover her sudden discomfort, she went over to the large stone fireplace. The mantel held an impressive array of tall trophies, plaques and some of the gem-encrusted belt buckles he'd won over the years. They were the only personal items in the room, and she suspected that if she roamed through the rest of the house, she wouldn't find any more.

This was the last of them, she realized sadly. The ones that meant so much to him, even in his darkest hour he couldn't bear to sell them. Picking up one of the buckles, she read the year and smiled. "I remember this one. It was your first regional rodeo."

"Yours, too," he reminded her, coming over to stand beside her. "We really kicked it that year, didn't we?"

"Yeah, we did," she recalled, laughing. "And Sadie nailed one of the clowns when he got too close. It didn't take them long to figure out that pretty as she is, she doesn't put up with any nonsense."

"Kinda like her owner."

"Better watch it, cowboy. That sounded dangerously like a compliment."

"It was," he conceded, adding a mischievous grin. "But I promise to be more careful from now on."

She wasn't quite sure what he meant by that, but she felt on steadier ground now, so she opted to let the comment go. Setting the buckle in its spot, she looked over the rest of his collection, which was much smaller than it used to be. "Some of these have genuine diamonds and gems on them. You could have gotten a lot for them, so why did you keep them?"

"These are all my firsts," he explained in a voice that sounded way too humble for the cocky rider she once knew. "That makes 'em special."

A framed photo in the center of the display caught her eye, and she pulled it from its spot for a closer look. Spinning it so he could see it, she said, "This is us at Cheyenne Frontier Days, ten years ago."

He simply nodded, and after waiting a few seconds, she realized that he wasn't going to say anything about it. Irked by his suddenly uncooperative attitude, she glared up at him. "What's it doing in with your favorite trophies? Is that how you think of me?"

"You know better than that," he shot back, narrowing his own eyes right back to her. "It was the first time we went there to compete instead of watch, and I had a great time."

"We both lost in the first round."

"Not me." After a few moments, he grinned. "You don't remember, do you?"

"Remember what?"

"That was when you told me you loved me." Taking the picture from her, he set it back in the place of honor on his mantel and swung a melancholy gaze back to her. "I've had a lot of firsts, but that one was extra special, because it was you."

The softness in his mellow voice was doing strange things to her stomach, and she fought against it with a dose of common sense. "I'm sure you've heard that plenty of times since then."

"You can believe whatever you want, MJ. But in spite of the fact that I messed everything up at the end, what we had together meant a lot to me."

"Then why?" she heard herself ask. She hadn't intended to confront him about his motive for leaving now—or ever—but suddenly, she had to know. "If you loved me so much, why did you just take off like that?"

Raking a hand through his damp hair, he stared at the collection of mementoes before looking at her. In his eyes, she saw a combination of remorse and anguish that would have shredded a heart much harder than hers.

"Fear."

She snorted at the idea of it. "You've never been afraid of anything."

"That night, I was." Pulling away from her, he began pacing around the empty room as if searching for a way to explain his baffling decision to her. "It sounds crazy, but after I dropped you off at your place, it hit me that if we kept going the way we were, we'd end up married."

"Sounds awful," she scoffed, unable to see the problem. "And considering that you were so hot to have a family, and I was pregnant at the time, if you'd hung around, you would've had everything you wanted."

Ty hesitated, which was unlike him. Normally, he jumped first and thought about it later. His unusual show of caution gave her the impression that he was about to share something that he'd never told anyone else.

"I did want a family." Sighing, he fixed her with a woeful look. "But I didn't want a family like the one I grew up in. Mom fussed about every little thing, and Dad worked all the time just to get away from her. When they were together, all they did was fight."

"Yeah, I remember hearing them a few times when we were out on the porch."

"We weren't allowed to have pets in the house, 'cause they were too messy. The horses were okay, because Robby and I took care of them, and they never came inside. So we spent all our time outside 'cause that's where we could act like kids and not get in trouble for it."

He wasn't explaining himself all that

clearly, but Morgan knew him well enough to be able to fill in the blanks.

"So you were afraid we'd end up like that?" He nodded slowly, and she wanted to scream. "How on earth could you think that? I'm so much not like your mother, we could've come from different planets. And while we're on the subject of fighting, us Whittakers are pros at it. What made you think we were the perfect family?"

"You weren't, but you loved each other, and when something was wrong, you always worked it out."

"What made you believe that you and I wouldn't figure out how to handle things the same way?"

"Neither one of us is good at compromising." Now that he'd finally hit the crux of what he'd been trying to say, he actually looked relieved. "I worried that we'd make each other miserable, and then our kids would grow up the same way I did. I didn't want that to happen, so I left. I know it was cowardly, but I didn't know what else to do."

"Talk to me?" she suggested, her temper beginning to simmer as if his betrayal had happened yesterday. "Tell me how you were feeling? Or maybe leave me a note so I didn't have to keep wondering what went wrong?

Any of those would've been better than just disappearing that way."

"That occurred to me a few months later, but by then I was afraid it was too late to make things right."

He had a point there, she acknowledged with a mental sigh. Pregnant and unable to ride, she'd returned home and spent the final four months of her difficult pregnancy on strict bed rest. Doing everything in her power to ensure that her twins were born healthy. She'd hated him then, for being able to go on with his life as if nothing had happened.

It had never occurred to her that he might regret what he'd done. The man in front of her with his heart on his sleeve wasn't the same guy she'd been picturing all this time. This was the Ty she remembered, the boy who was always coming up with something fun to do, the teenager who helped her perfect her calf-roping technique for her junior rodeo competitions.

The young man who kissed her in the moonlight one evening and promised her the stars.

Sweet as that image was, it conflicted with the one she'd formed of him over the years that he'd been gone. Was it possible that the humbling nature of his accident had gentled his arrogant streak? Since his apology that first day she saw him in town, she'd been struggling to reconcile her bitter memories with the amiable man who was trying to rebuild his life from the ground up.

Bewildered by the conflicting emotions swirling through her, she firmly shut them down and got practical. Going into the kitchen, she found some ibuprofen in the cupboard and filled a glass with water. Handing them over the pass-through, she simply said, "Take those."

Judging by his grimace, he'd been expecting her to say something about his very personal revelation. She felt a twinge of guilt for disappointing him, but she didn't know how she felt about it all. Until she did, she wasn't about to say something she'd end up regretting later. He followed her order without complaint, draining the glass before setting it on the framed opening.

"Thanks for bringing me home," he said politely, as if they were strangers. "I can manage from here."

"Take it easy, and if you need anything, just call."

That got her another woeful look, but he didn't say anything else. That was good, she decided as she walked through the front door and out to the truck. Because she wasn't sure she could give him any more than she already had. Not long ago, she'd have known for certain that having some kind of future relationship with Ty Wilkins would never happen.

But now that she finally understood the truth of what had driven him away from her, she could feel her resolve starting to waver. Doubting herself aggravated her to no end, and unfortunately she had a feeling that she was in for a long bout of it.

Chapter Seven

W hat was he going to do?

It had been a few days since his foolish attempt at reliving his ranching glory days, and Ty's back finally felt good enough for him to walk more than a few yards. He'd been going stir-crazy cooped up at home and was just about giddy to be breaking up the monotony with a drive into town. It was summer, he reasoned, and the weather had brought out the sort of bright, endless blue that had given Montana its nickname of Big Sky Country. This was his favorite time of year, and he knew that should be more than enough to make him happy.

Instead, he was growing more worried by the day. He didn't need much money to keep Clyde and himself going, but his modest savings wouldn't last more than a few months if he had to keep dipping into it to pay their everyday living expenses. He needed a job that would at least help to keep him afloat until he could figure out a better long-term strategy.

While he tried to think positive, JD's comment from a few weeks ago echoed in his mind.

Starting over ain't easy, but it might go better if you get a little help once in a while.

The trouble was, Ty was used to taking care of himself, running things his own way without having to rely on anyone else. Admitting that he might not be able to live that way anymore was proving to be more difficult than he could have ever imagined during his carefree rodeo days.

"Mornin', Ty!"

Through the open window of his truck, he heard the greeting as he drove through town. He couldn't see who'd yelled his name, but he raised his hand in reply anyway. That was how it went all the way down Main Street, one person after another, until someone actually stepped into the empty street and held out his arms to make Ty stop.

"Perry Thompson?" he asked, easily recognizing their high school's track star even after all these years. Tall and lean, he had the look of a man who'd made it a point to stay in shape as he matured. "What're you doin' here? Last I heard, you were running one of those ecotourism resorts in Hawaii."

"Last I heard, you were tearing up the southwestern rodeo circuit," his old buddy shot back with a good-natured grin. Wiggling his left hand, he proved his point with an unmistakable glint of gold. "Things change."

Ty caught on to the upbeat tone and chuckled. "What's her name?"

"Kailani." Standing in the middle of the street as if it happened every day, Perry took out his phone and showed Ty the picture of a lovely Polynesian woman on a beach, holding a baby with her coloring and Perry's blue eyes. "We got married on Maui last fall and moved back here just after that. She owns the Ohana Bakery you passed on your way into town. The little one is Lea. She'll be a year old in January."

"They're both beautiful. Congrats, man." Ty handed the phone back, feeling a pang of envy for his friend. It must be nice to have all the pieces of your life in place and be able to look forward to the future instead of dreading what it might hold.

"Thanks." The new father tucked his phone away and rested his elbows on the window frame of the pickup. "What's up with you?"

"I'm out at the little ranch I bought from my parents a few years back."

Perry tilted his head with a chiding look. "You're not fooling me, dude. I know what happened with you and that bull. We all do."

Wonderful, Ty thought with a mental groan. Not that he'd expected anything different, but since no one beyond the Whittakers had mentioned it to him, he'd allowed himself to believe that the residents of his hometown were too preoccupied with the impending development issue to pay much attention to his predicament. Normally, he hated being so wrong about something, but this time, he was surprised to find that he didn't mind so much. In fact, he found it comforting to know that even though he hadn't seen his hometown folks in a while, they still cared about him.

Another car finally turned onto Main Street, and he said, "It's been good to see you, but I'd best get outta the way."

To his surprise, Perry motioned for him to wait and climbed into the cab beside him. "I have something to ask you, if you've got time."

"Dude," he replied, echoing his friend's earlier comment, "these days I have nothin' but time."

"Actually, I'm glad to hear that," Perry said

as they pulled into one of the angled parking spots that lined the modest business district.

About six blocks in length, it boasted shops that sold all the necessities of life in Mustang Ridge. Whether you needed a new saddle, tractor parts or repairs on your computer, the storekeepers pretty much had you covered. At the far end, like a tattered soldier keeping watch over the village, stood the farm store and grain elevator that had the distinction of being the first commercial building constructed in the town. Big Sky Feed and Seed had seen better days, but JD had told him that it still did a thriving business, mostly because it was the only one of its kind within twenty miles.

The former owner had given him his first job hauling feed when Ty was fourteen, he recalled fondly. Not so fondly, it was also where he'd run across Morgan when he first got back to town a few weeks ago, and she threw his heartfelt apology back in his face. A lot had happened since then, but she still hadn't forgiven him.

Now that he'd finally come clean about the reason for him breaking things off with her, he wasn't sure where he stood with her. Come to think of it, that was how he'd always felt around the mystifying woman who'd stolen his heart so long ago. If only he could come up with a way to get that part of him back, he might finally be able to get on with his life.

"So," he began, shifting in his seat to face his passenger squarely, "why are you glad to hear I've got nothing to do?"

"I'm swamped at the store, and two of my summer employees just bolted for the new amusement park they built about ten miles from here. I could really use a reliable counter person who's good with customers and won't flake out on me in the middle of my busiest season."

That sounded like something he could manage. While he'd prefer to work outside, Ty understood that he had to be practical about the physical limitations he now had. His afternoon running fence with the Whittakers had made it painfully clear that his days of hands-on ranching were behind him.

"I appreciate you thinking of me," he said with a grin. "What kind of business is it?"

Perry chuckled at that. "Sorry, I forgot you've been gone so long. I own the feed store now, bought it off Mr. Peters before he and his wife retired and moved to Phoenix. Remember how we used to run forklift races after he left for the day?"

"Yeah, I do," Ty commented, grinning at

the memory. "As a matter of fact, I think I'm still up by one."

"Not a chance. I was the fourteen-and-under modified racing champ, remember?"

"That was cars," Ty reminded him good-naturedly, tapping his chest proudly. "I was the best forklift driver in Mustang Ridge."

"Come to work for me, and we'll settle for once and all who's better."

"You're gonna pay me even if I beat you, right?"

"That depends. When can you start?"

Ty didn't even hesitate. "How 'bout now?"

Perry held out his hand, and they shook to seal their deal. And, just like that, Ty had the job he'd been so worried about finding.

It didn't take him long to reorient himself in his old workplace. Perry had kept things pretty much the way they'd been for the past forty years, which Ty thought was wise. The residents of this stubbornly small town were pretty set in their ways, and they hated change of any kind. He had added in a long counter with stools near the register, outfitted with a series of bins labeled with stickers imprinted with Ohana Bakery's ocean-view logo. They held fresh treats from his wife's bakery and at the end was a coffee bar that would make any big-city boutique proud.

"This is cool," Ty approved, scanning the setup to make sure he'd be able to operate it if needed.

"Kailani's idea," Perry admitted sheepishly. "I didn't want all this, but she convinced me to try it for a month. Customers liked it so much, they went down the street to compliment her on the idea. I ate crow for a week."

Ty had never enjoyed the taste of crow himself, and he sympathized with his buddy's plight. A few minutes later, his employee reorientation was interrupted by the sound of jangling bells over the entry door. Glancing over to see who'd come in, he was surprised to see Morgan step inside, scowling while she listened to something on her phone. He couldn't imagine who could be causing that look, but Ty was grateful that at least this time it wasn't him.

"You've got the hang of it now," Perry announced, clearly sensing that it was time to make himself scarce. "I'll be on the loading dock if you need me."

Ty's new boss gave him a quick wink on his way out, which didn't make any sense. Curious as he was, Ty had a feeling he'd rather not know the reason for it. It was bound to be personal, or embarrassing, or both. While he was wondering about Perry's odd behavior, Morgan's expression went from furious to resigned, and she slid her phone into a back pocket of her jeans with a quiet sigh.

"Somethin' wrong?" he asked, meeting her gaze across the counter.

"Things don't always go your way, y'know?" Her eyes snagged on the hand-lettered name tag Perry had whipped up for him, and she tilted her head in confusion. "When did you start working here?"

Ty angled his wrist to check a nonexistent watch. "About half an hour ago. I'm new, so go easy on me."

"Okay," she agreed, her grim look giving way to a cute smile that reminded him of Hannah. Settling onto a stool, she took a chocolate-filled croissant from the bin, holding it up so he could see it. "This and a large coffee loaded with cream and sugar, please."

Some things never changed, he mused while he got her order ready. Morgan had always loved the kick of coffee, but not the taste. For someone whose life had been turned upside down over the past year, Ty found it soothing to know that some of the things he remembered were still the same.

Setting the cup in front of her, he decided to take a run at finding out what was upsetting the normally self-confident barrel racer.

Grabbing a damp towel, he made a show of wiping down the counter. "Little early for that much chocolate, isn't it?"

"Not today." Blowing on her coffee, she took a sip before downing half of the croissant in a single bite. Closing her eyes, she sighed in approval. "I don't know how she does it, but I'm convinced that if Kailani put her mind to it, she could solve most of our problems in that kitchen of hers."

Ty knew a dodge when he heard one, and he decided to play along. "There used to be a pizza place in there, and before that it was a bookstore. When did she take over the property?"

"About six months ago. She loves to cook, and being the boss means she can bring the baby to work with her. Lea's just about the cutest little bundle of smiles and laughter you ever saw."

"Yeah, I saw a picture of the two of 'em. Looks to me like Perry struck gold in Hawaii."

Morgan nodded her agreement and helped herself to another pastry. When she took money out to pay for it, he waved her off. "I got this one."

"Meaning you feel sorry for me."

The dejected tone in her voice made him

want to step in and fix whatever had gone wrong for her. But he knew perfectly well that she wouldn't accept his help, so he grinned and shook his head. "Meaning it's slow this morning, and I like having company at the counter instead of standing around looking for stuff to do."

"Even if it's me."

Especially if it's you, he nearly blurted out before his brain kicked in and stopped him. "Aw, you're not so bad. Everyone has an off day once in a while."

"Thanks. Believe it or not, that's one of the nicest things I've heard all week."

It wasn't like her to be so open about her feelings—good or bad—and her demeanor was really starting to worry him. Settling on a stool, he leaned forward on his elbows so they could talk more quietly. "Morgan, I know I'm probably not your first choice for confiding in, but if you wanna talk about whatever's going on, I'm happy to listen."

She eyed him for several long, uncomfortable moments, then swallowed some more coffee as if seeking time to make her choice. Patience wasn't his strong point, and all the boot-dragging made him want to hurry her along. But he recognized that pressuring her wouldn't get him anywhere, and would only cause her to pull even further away from him. She might have stopped freezing him out, but that was only the first step of many.

Rebuilding her trust in him was going to take careful, consistent effort on his part. It wouldn't be easy, but the image of the two of them raising their daughters as co-parents floated into his mind, encouraging him to remain quiet.

"Dad and I ran the numbers on our trip to Washington," she began hesitantly, her grimace making it clear they weren't good. "Two flights, two hotel rooms for at least two nights. It's gonna be way more than the conservancy can afford right now. We need to hire a lawyer, maybe even two, to push through the temporary injunction against Cartwright Energy. When we first started, folks volunteered their time to get the word out and circulate petitions around the area. Now it's getting expensive, and we have to spend our money where it will do the most good."

Her comment about local residents donating their time got his wheels spinning, and he hunted around under the counter for something that might help. When he found a large empty glass jar, he set it on the counter in front of her.

"What's that for?" she asked, clearly lost.

"Donations." Grabbing a roll of wide masking tape, he stretched a length of it out on the glass countertop and handed her a permanent marker. "You've got better handwriting than me. You label it. I'll make sure customers see it. I don't doubt that Kailani would do the same, and so would any of the business owners in town who want to protect our wide-open spaces. A little here, a little there, who knows? We just might get enough so we can stay in a hotel instead of camping out in a park near the White House."

She laughed at the ridiculous suggestion. "It's the nation's capital, Ty. With security the way it is now, we couldn't really do that."

Her laughter inspired him, and he grinned. "If we rounded up some people and had a good, old-fashioned barbecue and sing-along, just think how much publicity we'd get."

"Sure, right before they hauled us off to jail."

It wouldn't be his first trip there, but he decided to keep that less-than-stellar detail about his past to himself. Instead, he chuckled. "Last I knew, this was America, and I can camp anywhere I want."

Shaking her head, the smile she gave him was more approving than not. "You're really getting into this rebel with a cause thing, aren't you?"

"Now, that's downright insulting," he retorted, adopting a miffed attitude to keep their lighthearted discussion going. "The sticker in the window of my truck says I'm an official member of the Mustang Ridge Conservancy. That and the paperwork I'm doing with JD makes me a devoted environmentalist."

"You're a devoted something, anyway," she scoffed, finishing her coffee before tossing the cup into the bin beside the register. "Fun as this has been, I really do need a few things before I head back to the ranch."

As she slid from her stool and walked into the stacks, his impulse was to follow after her. But it occurred to him that if he did that, she'd feel crowded, so he forced himself to stay where he was. "Let me know if you need a hand with anything."

Turning back, she rewarded him with an appreciative smile. "Thanks, I will."

That view of her was the one he wanted so desperately, Ty realized. Since their soul-bearing conversation, he'd run all kinds of scenarios for them through his head. Most of them were bad, and he'd finally given up trying to work things out mentally. Fearing that he'd lost any ground he'd made up, he'd dreaded seeing her again and finding out that she'd decided to punt him back to where he started.

Then, to his surprise, he heard her calling his name. When he went over to see what she wanted, she met him with a look that was equal parts uncertain and determined. It was as if she was about to do something she wasn't thrilled about but knew it had to be done anyway.

Glancing around, she stepped closer and spoke quietly. "I saw how you looked when we were talking about Perry's little girl."

Ty wasn't sure where this was headed, but he saw no sense in denying it. "Families— good ones—always get to me, I guess. Mine wasn't the best, and I've always wanted a chance at being part of something better."

"I know." Pausing, she took in a hesitant breath before continuing. "You're really great with Allie and Hannah, and you've made it plain that you want to be part of their lives. I'd be okay with that on one condition."

Ty's heart launched itself into his throat. This was the very thing he'd been praying for, although he was still awkward at it since he wasn't a pro at talking to the Almighty just yet. "Name it."

"You're not allowed to tell them that you're their father."

"They have to find out sometime."

"I know that," she allowed grimly, as if it was the last thing on earth she wanted to consider. "But now isn't the time. I'll decide when it's right, not you."

He wasn't crazy about deceiving his daughters, but yesterday he couldn't have imagined getting even this much of a concession from Morgan. If this was what she was willing to give him, he saw no option other than to go along. "Then I accept your condition. Thank you."

"You're welcome." She turned partially before looking back to nail him with a warning glare. "Don't make me regret it."

You didn't have to be a genius to understand that she was referring to the last time he'd let her down. Although the reminder stung, he couldn't blame her for it. "I won't."

His simple response seemed to satisfy her, and she left him behind while she made her way toward the back of the store.

Now that he had Morgan's official go-ahead to spend time with his girls, Ty felt some of the worry that had been weighing him down leave his shoulders. Standing tall was a lot easier when you weren't hauling all your past mistakes around with you.

"Mommy?"

Tying a bright blue ribbon to the end of Allie's single French braid, Morgan replied, "Yes, sweetie?"

"Can we bring Ty to church?"

Whoa, was Morgan's first thought. Close behind it was the knowledge that Allie didn't often come up with ideas like this one, and her heart brightened at the thought that her reserved girl was beginning to gain some social confidence. That her proposal involved Ty Wilkins didn't thrill her, but she'd take it. Allie seldom asked for anything, and when she did, Morgan did everything in her power to grant her wish. "I'm not sure he's up yet, but we can stop by on our way and ask him."

"He's really nice," Hannah chimed in while she tied her good shoes. "He remembers the names of all my dolls, and I only had to tell him once. Grandpa calls them all doll face."

Morgan laughed at her father's clever solution for keeping his granddaughter happy without having to memorize nearly thirty names. And even though she knew Ty's attentiveness had an ulterior motive behind it, she had to admire his willingness to put in that kind of effort to make a six-year-old doll mama happy.

She finished her hair duty with the double ponytails Hannah had requested, then stood and brushed her hands off. They both looked perfect to her, Allie in pale blue chambray and Hannah in blue calico that gave her the appearance of being some long-ago prairie girl. "All done. Why don't you two go have breakfast with Grandpa while I get ready?"

"Mommy?"

Hunkering down, she got on the same level as her sweet, shy girl. "Yes, Allie?"

"Why do you always go last?"

At first, she didn't understand the question. Then it dawned on her that it was true. Her girls came first, then her family, then the ranch. And now, the conservancy. During her increasingly rare spare time, she'd tack up Sadie and go for a run, always ending up at the mustangs' valley. She'd start out admiring them, but always ended up counting them, assessing their condition and whether the public land they occupied provided enough space for their growing numbers.

Someday, she hoped they'd be able to truly run free again, safely roaming wherever they wanted the way God had always intended. But for now...

When Morgan registered that her daughters were staring at her, she realized that—once again—her mind had escaped her control and wandered off on its own. Too bad there wasn't a way for her to fence that in, too, she thought wryly.

"Sorry, girls, I got distracted. Mommies have a lot of stuff to think about."

"You need a vacation," Hannah suggested helpfully, sounding like an adorable commercial for getting away. "Miss Grainger is going to the Grand Canyon with her dog, and they're going to hike to the bottom to see what's there. You should take Skye somewhere fun."

Morgan didn't have the time or money for adventures, but she appreciated the thought. "I'll think about it," she promised, giving them each a quick hug. "For now, though, I'll go get myself ready for church."

"And then we'll get Ty," Allie reminded her earnestly.

"We'll give it a shot, anyway," Morgan agreed as she stood up. "I'll be down in a few minutes."

After hurrying through her bare-bones morning routine, Morgan chose the blue option of the two dresses she owned and dug through her collection of boots for a pair of shoes to wear. Again, she only had two, different versions of the same style she'd found in a bargain bin a few years ago. Like the dresses, she seldom wore them, and they ended up jumbled into the pile she tossed into her closet when she didn't have an opportunity to put things away. Which was most days.

Finally, she found two flats and gladly stepped into them before hurrying downstairs. Dad and the girls were already standing by the front door, so she grabbed a muffin from the platter on the table and followed them outside.

After making sure the girls were buckled into the backseat of her father's trusty old SUV, Morgan got in beside him and did the same. While she was setting her purse on the floor near her feet, she was horrified by what she saw.

One black shoe and one navy.

Dad glanced over with a frown before focusing on the view out the windshield. "Something wrong?"

"I forgot something, but it's no big deal."

"Allie told me we're stopping to pick up Ty," he went on as they turned from their driveway into his. "I didn't remember him being the religious type."

She had no idea what type he was these days, so Morgan casually said, "The girls wanted to invite him."

Her father hmmed in response but didn't say anything more. They found Ty sitting in a willow chair on his front porch, boots crossed on the railing while he watched them drive in. Dad didn't seem inclined to leave the truck, so Morgan opened her door.

"Us, too, Mommy!" Hannah insisted, bolting from her seat with Allie close behind. "It was our idea, and we want to ask him."

They were running late as it was, but Morgan swallowed her protest because this detour seemed so important to her daughters. They were trying to rope in a lost sheep, after all. Certainly God could forgive them for being a few minutes late to church.

Clearly surprised to see the three of them, Ty got to his feet with a bright grin. "Mornin', ladies. Where are you headed lookin' so pretty?"

"Church," Allie replied instantly, which amazed Morgan. The timid child seldom spoke first, usually letting Hannah take the lead in a conversation. It was another sign of how much this errand meant to her. Her impulsive approach seemed to falter, though, and Morgan braced herself for the withdrawal that typically followed.

To her astonishment, Ty went down on a knee to put him on Allie's level, just the way Morgan did. The kind, compassionate gesture did something strange to her heart, and she took a deep breath to regain her usual composure.

"You like church?" he asked her in the gentle voice Morgan had heard him use with skittish horses. When Allie nodded, he smiled. "What do you like best about it?"

"Singing."

Now, he shifted his eyes to Hannah, who'd been hanging back to give her sister the spotlight. "And what do you like best?"

"Sunday school. We get to do art projects and have cookies."

Ty chuckled. "I like cookies. Chocolate chip are my favorite."

"Me, too," she agreed brightly. "Mommy likes oatmeal."

Those hazel eyes drifted up to meet Morgan's, a fond twinkle warming the flecks of gold. "I remember."

In that single moment, it felt as if nothing had ever gone wrong between them. They were back in their good times, when it seemed like their love for each other would always be enough to get them through any obstacle life could throw at them. For one brief moment, Morgan almost believed they could have that again.

Almost.

Chiding herself for being so foolish, she got practical. "We're running late, so hop in if you want a ride."

"Thanks. That'd be great."

This time, Morgan gave him the front seat and she shared the back with the girls. Thankfully, Dad kept Ty well occupied on the way into town, which left her with nothing to do other than enjoy the view rolling past the open windows. Mustang Ridge closed down on Sundays, so the only traffic was headed toward one of the three churches clustered around the town square.

In the center of the green space stood a monument to area soldiers who'd fallen since the Civil War, which had occurred long before Montana earned its statehood in 1889. Morgan had always thought it was considerate of the statue's builders to include those long-ago infantrymen who'd died far from home defending the freedom they valued above everything.

In direct contrast to the somber message of the monument, on the side nearest the street was the playground that the town had funded and added to over the years. What had started as a few swings and slides had blossomed into a sturdy kid-centered compound with everything from rope nets to swaying bridges.

Over the top of it all was the donation from the historical society: a reproduction Conestoga wagon and two life-size wooden oxen. It gave the fun area a rustic Montanan flair, and seeing it up there always made Morgan smile.

Once they'd all piled out of the SUV and were headed up the front steps, Ty caught her elbow and tugged her aside.

"Hate to tell you this," he murmured, "but you've got two different shoes on."

Ordinarily, having him find fault with her for anything would've gotten her back up. But it was Sunday, so she bit her tongue and rolled her eyes. "I know. By the time I noticed, it was too late to go back and change."

"You always hated being late," he commented as they followed Dad and the girls into the small sanctuary.

"It's rude," she shot back instinctively, wishing she'd just pretended she hadn't noticed the problem herself. Honesty might be the best policy, but sometimes it was just a hassle.

"You've never had trouble matching up

your boots," he pointed out, clearly refusing to let the matter drop. "Maybe you could try rubber banding your shoes together to make things easier on yourself."

Considering the source, it wasn't the worst suggestion she'd ever heard. She realized that he was actually trying to be helpful, so she let her annoyance go with a quiet breath. "That's a good idea. I'll give it a try."

It took a few minutes to get to their seats, since everyone kept stopping them to talk about something or other. Between the horses and cattle on the ranch, there was plenty to discuss, but lately more people wanted an update on the conservancy's efforts. Some wanted to help, others to make it plain to her that they opposed what she was attempting to do. One thing they all had in common, though. A strong opinion. Whether she agreed with them or not, she had to admire folks who had the guts to take a stand and refuse to shrink from a challenge.

"Man, this energy thing has really taken over the town," Ty muttered, standing in the aisle to let the girls go ahead of him to sit near Jessie. "At the feed store, it's almost as popular a topic as the weather."

"People care about what happens here," Morgan reminded him as she took a children's Bible from the rack and passed it down for Allie and Hannah to share.

"Guess I kinda forgot what that's like."

Morgan glanced up at him and caught the pensive expression clouding his usually easy-going features. Was it really possible that the reckless cowboy she'd known for most of her life was maturing into the kind of thoughtful, caring man she could depend on? As she thought back over the weeks since he first reappeared, she couldn't deny that he'd changed. Whether it was the injuries he'd suffered, or that he was simply mellowing with time, she couldn't say for certain.

But he was definitely a different guy than the one who'd walked away from her all those years ago. Now that she had an explanation for his vanishing act, she found herself feeling something for him that she hadn't anticipated. Understanding.

"It's nice to be around people like that," she agreed. "Being a gypsy on the rodeo circuit was fun, but being grounded here works for me, too. Except when I can't find my other shoe," she added with a grimace.

"If that's your worst problem today, I'd say you're doing just fine."

He added an encouraging smile, and she

couldn't help returning the gesture. "You know all about tough days, don't you?"

"I try not to think about it too much, but yeah, I've had my share."

More than his share, she suspected, although she respected his attempt to make his ordeal seem more manageable than it must have felt at the time. Especially when he was on his own, far from Mustang Ridge, being cared for by strangers. Competent and compassionate, but strangers all the same. When she'd been in trouble, she'd headed straight for the ranch and the family she knew would love and support her, no matter what.

Ty hadn't had much of that, she realized sadly, even when his parents were still together. As deeply as he'd hurt her when he left, it occurred to her that he'd suffered nearly as much. For all these years, she'd assumed that he'd gone on to something—and someone—else that made him happy.

Not long ago, knowing that his decision had made him miserable would have given her some grim satisfaction. But now, it just made her wistful for what might have been.

Ty had never been one for church.

Summer Sundays were for sleeping in, followed by long rides and watching baseball on TV while he plowed his way through the week's laundry and chores. While he was growing up, his family attended services at Easter and Christmas, more as a form of being counted in God's flock than anything else. As a result, he didn't have an opinion one way or the other on religion. If it worked for you, that was great. If not, that was fine, too.

But as he sat in that sunny chapel that he'd barely known during his younger days, listening to the Sunday school's adorable rendition of "Jesus Loves Me," he got a different view of the place and what it meant to them. He didn't know any of the other kids standing up there, but they looked like a group of cherubs, dressed in their nicest clothes, doing their best to stay on key.

His daughters caught his attention, looking like miniature Morgans in their pretty blue dresses, with sunshine streaming in from the tall windows to light their faces. He'd just started getting acquainted with them, but they amazed him more every day. Hannah with her quick mind and army of dolls, Allie with her love of animals and incredible talent for drawing them. They truly were the best of Morgan and him, blended into two incredible children who deserved every bit of good that life could give them.

They were his girls, he mused sadly, but they didn't know it. When Morgan had first made her proposal allowing him to spend time with them, he'd quickly agreed, believing that the limited arrangement would be enough for him. But as the weeks had worn on, it had become more obvious to him that being "good neighbor Ty" wasn't going to cut it.

They were his children, and he wanted to be their father. All the way, for good or bad, because the family he'd always wanted was standing only a few yards away, just waiting for him to step up and claim them.

The trouble was Morgan. She'd made it painfully clear how she felt about that possibility, so for now at least, he put his longing aside and applauded while the kids took their bows before following their teacher downstairs for Sunday school.

"Joining the kids for cookies?" Morgan whispered while the pastor got organized at his lectern.

The guy Ty once was would've jumped at the opportunity to go hang out with the kids and enjoy some snacks. But he stopped himself. If he was going to prove to her that he was in fact "father material," it was time to start acting like a grown-up. Most of the time, anyway. "I think I'll hear what Pastor Bartlett has to say this morning."

She didn't respond, but the stunned look on her face was priceless. After a moment, it softened into something he hadn't seen from her in so long, he'd forgotten what it looked like. Respect.

Feeling proud of himself for surprising the very unpredictable Morgan Whittaker, Ty settled back and prepared a few tricks he'd learned for keeping himself awake.

When Pastor Bartlett left the raised lectern area and sat down on the top step of the little stage, though, Ty realized he might have misjudged the modest-looking man. Resting his elbows on his knees, he sent a look through the packed church, pausing here and there to connect with people along the way. And when he began to speak, Ty felt himself leaning forward to catch whatever this quiet, patient man had to say.

"Sometimes," he began in a pretty unremarkable manner, "we make mistakes. We're human, and life can seem pretty random. When we get caught off guard, especially by circumstances not of our own making, we get rattled and make choices we regret later on.

I know, because I've done that kind of thing myself. On occasion, I've been guilty of assuming that I knew what was best for other people, rather than allowing them to find their own way."

As the preacher went on to describe some of his other faults, Ty noticed folks around him nodding slightly, as if his humble confession reminded them of their own past behavior. With Morgan sitting beside him, his own mind flashed back to the day he determined that he wasn't good enough for her and took off. Thinking he was doing her a favor, protecting her from a lifetime of remorse, in truth he'd taken away her God-given right to choose for herself what she wanted.

And in a moment of inspiration, he understood why she'd been so angry with him for so long. Ending their relationship should have been *their* decision, not his alone. If only he'd talked it through with her, they might have been able to work things out. And he'd be sitting here in church with the family he'd always longed to have, instead of feeling like an arrogant fool.

While he was silently berating himself, Pastor Bartlett threw out a bit of hope to Ty and anyone else feeling the way he was right now. Standing, the preacher smiled at the people gathered for the service. "The good news for us is that God understands why we stumble, and He waits for us to realize what we've done wrong. He doesn't abandon us, although it may feel like it at times. Like any good father, He stands ready to support us, if only we'll ask Him for His help. For some of us, that's tough because it requires us to look inside ourselves, acknowledge our failings and make changes to keep those things from happening again. It isn't easy, but I can promise you that the rewards are worth the effort."

Ty felt as if that sermon had been delivered to him personally, and judging by the reaction of many in the congregation, he wasn't the only one who'd gotten that message. Normally, he was more impressed by actions than words, but there was no denying that this particular man had a knack for speaking to people in a way they could not only understand but also relate to on a very personal level.

"Man," he murmured to Morgan as they stood for the final hymn, "he's good."

"He kept you awake," she retorted with a smirk.

Yeah, he did, Ty thought in admiration. But more than that, he'd reached a part of Ty that he hadn't thought much about before returning to his hometown like a beaten-down hound with his tail between his legs. He'd assumed that apologizing to Morgan would be the biggest thing he'd do before rebuilding his life, but now that he was getting to know his daughters, it was obvious that there was more to his journey than simply moving on.

Somehow, some way, he wanted the four of them to be a family. The challenge was getting Morgan to agree with him.

Chapter Eight

"Bye, Mommy," Hannah said, hugging Morgan before giving her a sunshine smile. "I know you'll do a great job telling those people in the government about our mustangs."

"Thanks, punkin. I'll try."

Allie hung back a little, and Morgan didn't prompt her to come say goodbye. It was mid-July, and somehow the conservancy had scraped together enough money for Ty and her to travel to Washington to present their case to Craig Barlowe's Natural Resources Committee. They'd be gone for three days, which right now felt like an eternity for her to be separated from her girls. Even though Dad, Ryan, Jessie and Ben were all pitching in to cover her absence, she hadn't been gone even a single night since they were born. The idea of taking a trip to the other side of the country without them was equal parts exciting and terrifying.

Once Hannah stepped back, Allie came forward, a rolled-up piece of drawing paper in her hands. Holding it up, she offered a rare smile of her own. "This is for you."

Morgan had learned to respond quickly to her reserved child, so she immediately said, "Thank you, sweetie." When she unrolled the page, she was truly amazed at the detailed picture her daughter had drawn of the wild herd that meant so much to all of them. Hunkering down, she pointed to one horse in particular. "Is this one your favorite?"

Allie nodded. "She's like Sadie."

"She is, and I would've recognized her anywhere. You did a great job."

"Hannah helped me with the flowers."

As always, Morgan thought as she gathered both of them into her arms. Holding them away, she said, "I'm so proud of my talented girls. We Whittakers make a great team, don't we?"

Both of them nodded, and she hugged them again, reluctant to let go. She had an important task ahead of her, but the fact that it was taking her away from them didn't sit well with her. The single-mom effect, she mused sadly. The endless tug-of-war that went on between motherhood and her obligation to the larger world was always tough to manage, but today it was even more so.

Aware that she was sliding into the quicksand of self-pity, she was actually relieved when Ty's truck pulled into the long driveway. Standing, she got a firm grip on her runaway emotions and shouldered her carry-on. Looking around the family circle who had come to see her off, she forced a confident tone. "That's my ride. I'll call you when we get there."

"Weather looks good all the way east," Dad told her, patting her shoulder. "You'll have lots of prayers behind you when you make your presentation to the committee tomorrow."

She knew he was behind that, and she smiled. "Thanks. That's good to know."

"Can't miss," Ryan assured her, his characteristic swagger on full display. "No matter where they're from, folks know a good argument when they hear one."

"Jessie and I are splitting rug rat duty," Ben reminded her, flashing her one of his cheerful country-boy grins. "You can count on us."

"I promise not to let him spoil them too much," her sister chimed in, lightly elbowing him in the ribs.

"That's what favorite uncles are for," he protested in an injured tone.

"'Favorite uncle'?" Ryan echoed in disdain. "Not in this lifetime, little brother."

They were all laughing when, to Morgan's surprise, Allie very clearly said, "No one's a favorite. We're a family."

It was incredible to hear one of the lessons she'd tried so hard to teach her daughters coming from one of them, and Morgan felt a rush of motherly pride. That it was Allie who'd made the announcement gave it even more meaning.

"Hey there," Ty greeted them as he sauntered over from his truck. "How're things over on this side of the fence today?"

It was the neighbor's greeting they'd been using with the Wilkinses since she could remember, and Dad smiled as they shook hands. "Sunny and warm. How 'bout you?"

"Same." Turning to Ben, he added, "Thanks for looking after Clyde while I'm gone. He's pretty mellow, so you shouldn't have a problem with him."

"Allie and Hannah are gonna help me, so he'll get plenty of attention. I get to take him out on the trail, right?"

"Sure, just be careful with him," Ty cautioned. "He loves to run, but he's not as young as he used to be."

"Got it."

Another round of hugs, and she and Ty were sitting in the cab of his pickup, headed for the highway. Morgan had a knot in her stomach, which only grew tighter as she ran down her mental checklist of all the things that could go wrong in the next three days, both at home and in Washington.

When she realized the truck was resting at an angle, she glanced over at Ty, who was staring at her for some reason. "What?"

"You okay?" he asked, concern darkening the green in his eyes.

"Sure. Why?"

"We've been driving for half an hour and you haven't said more than a dozen words. Something wrong?"

It irked her that even after all these years, he could still read her so well. But there was no point in denying her dread when he could see it clearly for himself, so she confided her misgivings to him.

"I haven't been gone a single night since I brought the twins home from the hospital when they were babies," she added. Then, because it felt good to share her anxiety with someone, she went on. "And the idea of facing all those politicians scares me to death. What if I can't make them understand how special Mustang Ridge is, and they decide not to help us?"

"I get that, but you don't have to do any of this by yourself. The girls are with your family, and Craig and I will be there when you speak to the committee. It's your show, but we'll be on hand if you need us."

"That's sweet, but—" A slow grin began working across his tanned features, and she frowned. "What?"

"You said I was sweet."

"Trying to make me feel better is sweet," she clarified tersely. "I would've said that to anyone."

"But you said it to me," he pointed out, shifting the truck into gear and pulling back onto the road. "I heard you."

"Whatever." Morgan wished she could convince him that he'd misunderstood her, but she doubted she could manage it. He'd think what he wanted to think, and there wasn't anything she could do about that. Unfortunately, a faint awareness in the back of her mind was pushing its way forward despite her efforts to keep it at bay.

Her wayward cowboy *was* being thoughtful, and not only to her. His warmth and understanding with their daughters still amazed her, especially the unexpected bond he'd managed to form with Allie. She was habitually cautious around strangers, but he'd found a way to connect with her on her own terms, all while making Hannah feel just as important.

To her great astonishment, Ty Wilkins was proving himself to be a really good dad. The man she'd once deemed "not father material" had matured into someone generous and patient, an engaged neighbor who Allie and Hannah grew fonder of every day. That didn't make them the traditional big, happy family that she'd always prayed for, she realized, but it was a lot closer than some people got.

"Y'know," Ty broke into her reverie in a casual way that sounded forced. Flicking a glance her way, he focused back on the road before continuing. "I've been curious about your mom. She hasn't been around, and no one talks about her. Is she okay?"

"I'd imagine so. She's living in Helena to be closer to her boyfriend."

It got so quiet, she could hear the hum of some mechanical flaw in the truck's engine. After about a mile of that, her traveling companion seemed to regain his usual cool. "That's awful, MJ. I'm sorry."

"I'm not," she snapped defensively, as she'd done so many times when someone had the gall to bring up her absent mother. "She's been gone a year, so we've all had time to adjust. If she doesn't want to be here, that's her choice. We're doing just fine without her."

He absorbed that calmly, then quietly said, "She just left, didn't she? No warning, no explanation."

"Yes. That's how cowards do things."

"Cowards like me, you mean?"

She hadn't been talking about him, but now that he mentioned it, that was how she'd felt back then. Not anymore, though, she realized with sudden clarity. Once he'd explained the reason behind his betrayal, her icy view of him had gradually thawed until she was able to imagine herself completely forgiving him someday. "I suppose so. But you were a lot younger, and we weren't married, so it was different."

"If I'd known you were pregnant, I would've stayed."

"But not for me," she commented, oddly without bitterness. It was more a statement of fact, but it felt good to say it out loud. "I wasn't enough for you."

"You were way more than enough for me,"

he corrected her with a grimace. "That was the problem. When my parents split up, they were horrible to each other. I loved you so much, it actually frightened me. I couldn't stand the thought that if something happened with us, you'd hate me the way they hated each other."

"I always thought you weren't afraid of anything."

"That's what I wanted everyone to think." His sheepish manner was so rare, she had a tough time believing he was the same brash guy who lived next door. "I guess I figured it was easier that way. No one bugs you if they believe you can handle anything that comes along."

Something in his tone hit home with her, and she realized it was the first time in the twenty-plus years they'd known each other that they'd ever had a conversation like this. "Were you scared after your accident?"

"Terrified. One doctor wasn't sure I'd ever walk again." Ty glanced over, the gold in his eyes glinting mischievously. "I fired him."

"Good for you," she approved immediately. "No one on this earth has a right to tell you what you're capable of except for you."

That earned her the bright, boyish grin

she'd always adored. "That's how I felt about it, too. The next one—who happened to be a woman, by the way—gave me a better opinion and when I was ready, she set me up with a top-notch rehab team. It was tough, and it seemed to take forever, but I'm upright on my own two feet, so it worked."

"But you're still riding, even though she told you not to. Are you sure that's the best idea?"

"Long as I stay in the saddle, I'll be okay." Now the grin took on some of its old arrogance. "I didn't earn all those fancy trophies by being easy to throw."

"You're an idiot," she announced, laughing at him. "But I get it. What's the point of having a life if you don't get to live it your way?"

"That's what I like most about you. You get me, even when no one else does."

"Is that a compliment?" she teased. "It's hard to tell."

"Yes, ma'am. Unless it made you mad, then I take it back."

Over the past few weeks, they'd gradually started bantering with each other the way they used to. Tentatively, as if they were leery of upsetting the delicate balance of their renewed friendship. This was how they used to talk, she acknowledged sadly, but until now they'd been careful not to push it too far.

For the first time since their unexpected reunion, the cold bitterness she'd been carrying for him warmed to the point where she could actually think about him and smile. She wasn't sure how to tell him that, so she reached over and rubbed his shoulder. "It didn't make me mad."

Sighing, he sent her a relieved look. "That's good, 'cause I'm runnin' outta ways to say *I'm sorry.*"

His confession made her realize that he'd been doing exactly that for nearly two months now, in one form or another. Maybe it was the beautiful day, or the fact that she was headed off on her first adventure since discovering she was pregnant seven years ago. Whatever the reason, it seemed like the right time to finally put their troubled past into a box and tie a ribbon on it.

"Ty?"

He glanced over at her. "Yeah?"

"You can stop apologizing to me. I forgive you."

"For?"

"Everything. You've been great ever since you got back, and you've convinced me that you never meant to hurt me."

After a moment, he took a deep breath, as if bracing himself for something he'd rather not do. "Does that mean you don't hate me anymore?"

"I never hated you," she admitted, as much to herself as to him. "It would've been easier if I did."

"I would've hated me."

"Well, you're not me."

"No, I'm not," he agreed in the humble tone she'd heard a lot more of lately. "Thanks, MJ. You don't know how much this means to me."

"You're welcome," she told him, then added, "and quit calling me MJ."

Laughing, he signaled for the airport exit. "Yes, ma'am."

Once they found a parking spot in the airport's crowded lot, the nice thing was that Ty carried her bag for her. The not-so-nice thing was the huge line at Security.

"I checked in online," she grumbled, leaning to the side to see why the mass of passengers was moving so slowly. "That's supposed to save you time at the airport."

"It does." Nodding back toward the ticket counters, he said, "Those folks all have bags to check, and they'll be waiting another half hour at least."

"At this rate, we could drive to DC quicker."

"Tell you what?" Grinning, he dangled his keys in front of her. "You take my truck and get started. I'll see you sometime next week."

His lighthearted comeback settled her nerves a bit, and she grudgingly smiled. "I wouldn't really drive all that way."

"Yeah," he agreed, putting the keys in his pocket. "You're smarter than that."

Feeling foolish, she felt she owed him an explanation for her childish behavior. "I really don't like planes."

"I remember. It's just about time for lunch at the ranch. Why don't you call the girls and see what they're up to?"

It was the perfect distraction for her, she realized as she pulled up the speed dial for home. It didn't escape her that he'd been the one to think of it. She put the phone on speaker so they could both hear about how Skye had taken off with Ben's roast beef sandwich and buried it under a rosebush in the backyard. Matilda had somehow gotten up into the rafters of Dad's office and was howling like a banshee although she refused to come down.

"Headin' out to get an extension ladder from the barn," Ryan grumbled. "Have a good flight."

"We will," Morgan replied, laughing as she

sent air kisses to her girls before hanging up. The time lapse had moved the line along, and they were up next. Setting her phone in a plastic tub, she slipped off her shoes and gave Ty her very best smile. "That was a great idea. Thanks."

"Anytime."

They grabbed some lunch at the food court and then found the gate for their flight, which was listed as delayed. Rather than get upset about it, she decided it was best to follow Ty's easygoing example and not let it get to her. Lounging beside her in the hard plastic seat, he stretched out his long, denim-clad legs and crossed his boots in a comfortable-looking pose. Then he tipped his signature cowboy hat down over his eyes and quickly dozed off.

The scene reminded her of trips they'd taken in the past, heading from one rodeo venue to another. Parking their pickups in massive truck stop lots, taking care of the horses before going into some diner or another for a meal. Hopscotching across the country had been fun, and she wouldn't trade those days for anything. They helped her appreciate what she had now that much more.

It was interesting how life worked out, she mused as she opened the mystery novel that Jessie had given her for Christmas two years ago. It had been a bestseller then, but she'd never found time to read it.

Now seemed like the perfect time. For a lot of things.

What a view.

Ty stood at the window of his hotel room, looking out over the bustling capital of the country in the waning light of day. Cars and pedestrians rushed past iconic buildings, hurrying by historical treasures on their way to wherever they were going. Their flight had been delayed twice, so the sightseeing tour they'd planned on would have to wait for another time.

Maybe they could bring Allie and Hannah with them, he thought, tucking his hands into the front pockets of his suit trousers while he envisioned the four of them hiking around the city, pausing to admire whatever interested the girls most. The Smithsonian had a section dedicated to children. It would make sense to start there. As much as that idea appealed to him, another element of his meandering thoughts intrigued him even more.

If it came to pass, it would be their first adventure as a family. One of many, he hoped, although he recognized that Morgan would have to go along with anything he proposed if it was going to move from dream to reality. And if he'd learned anything in the many years he'd known her, it was that the slender blonde with the incredible eyes was also rock stubborn when she made up her mind about something.

Then again, he added as he turned away from the window, so was he.

Strolling from the room, he went down the hallway and knocked on Morgan's door. After a few seconds, she opened it, and he felt his jaw hit the carpet. "Wow."

To his knowledge, she owned two dresses, which she alternated for Sundays at church. This one had to be new, and thanks to its feminine Western details, it was stunning. Made of some swirly peach-colored fabric, the buttoned-up bodice followed her curves perfectly, from lace-trimmed neckline to trim waist. The best part was that it accented the brilliant blue of her eyes, making them a color he'd never seen before.

Giving him a little smirk, she twirled for him in a very un-Morgan-like move. "Is this nice enough for that fancy restaurant Craig recommended?"

"And then some. I'm glad I've got a tie, or I'd be way underdressed." Fishing it out of his jacket pocket, he grinned. "Can you help me out?"

"When will you ever learn how to do that for yourself?"

"Well, I don't wear 'em much," he explained as he followed her into her room. "And I figure the last one'll get done up by the undertaker, so I won't care."

"You'll need one for our meeting tomorrow."

Always one step ahead of him, he thought with honest admiration. He'd dated plenty of beautiful women, but none of them had half her brains. "I'll just loosen this one and then tighten it back up in the morning."

"Okay, but what about all the formal occasions that are coming up?" she pressed, deftly whipping the knot together for him.

"Like what?"

"Weddings, other people's funerals, things like that."

She was getting at something, but he couldn't figure out what it was, so he shrugged. "I'll figure it out then, I guess."

"Same old Ty," she lamented, shaking her head. "Still winging your way through life."

Now he got it, and he chuckled. "Mostly, yeah. Keeps things interesting."

"Or chaotic," she corrected him primly,

picking up a small ivory-colored purse from the desk.

Angling a look at her, he couldn't keep back a grin. "Does that purse match your shoes?"

"Of course."

She'd made it sound as if it made perfect sense, and as he opened the door, he couldn't resist teasing her. "Seeing as you went to church one morning with two unmatched shoes, I'm impressed that you'd think of it."

Groaning, she rolled those gorgeous baby blues. "Don't remind me. Jessie brought that up when she insisted on helping me shop for this outfit. If I look put-together, it's because of her."

"'Cause your idea of a fashion statement is when your boots match your saddle."

That got him the kind of sassy grin that he hadn't seen nearly enough of lately. "Exactly. So, where are we going for dinner?"

As they made their way to the glass elevator, he said, "Believe it or not, it doesn't have a name, only a number—100."

"The number of people in the Senate," she commented with a nod. "Clever."

"Huh. I didn't think of that. You always were smarter than me."

The elevator doors opened, and she glanced up at him. "You really think so?"

"Always did."

She didn't say anything as they walked out the front door and onto the sidewalk. The restaurant was only a block away, and the warm evening air was a pleasant change after being cooped up in airports and planes most of the day. The maître d' had a table for them, which he informed them had been reserved and paid for by Craig.

"Cool," Ty said as he looked over the large, tasseled menu. "When I saw how swanky this place is, I was worried I'd be washing dishes or something."

Morgan laughed, and he grinned over at her. "Anyone ever tell you you've got the greatest laugh?"

"Not recently," she admitted, almost shyly. "I guess folks don't hear it all that much."

It wasn't like her to be so open about her emotions, and he wondered what had brought on the sudden confession. But he didn't want to spoil the evening by asking a lot of questions she probably wouldn't want to answer, so he opted for another approach. "If you have more fun, you'll laugh more."

"Is that your secret?"

"That, and not fretting over how to wrangle a tie."

She laughed again, and he congratulated

himself on averting a possibly difficult conversation neither one of them was eager to have. From appetizers through two enormous steaks, they chatted pleasantly about everything and nothing. It was the kind of evening they'd enjoyed so many times during their lifelong connection, and Ty hadn't realized how much he'd missed it until now.

"Excuse me," an unfamiliar man's voice said from behind him. "Are you Ty Wilkins?"

Glancing over his shoulder, Ty saw a middle-aged couple dressed in the classy, conservative manner that he'd noticed on pretty much everyone in the spacious dining room. Getting to his feet, he smiled at them. "Yes, sir, I am. Can I help you?"

He was flabbergasted when the man handed him a piece of paper and a sleek silver pen. "Would you mind giving us an autograph? We saw you compete in Austin a couple of years ago and became instant fans."

That was a new one. Usually, people who enjoyed watching him ride slapped him on the back and offered to buy him a drink. "Sure. Who should I make it out to?"

"Neil and Georgia Fitzpatrick," the woman prompted him. "And thank you so much."

"You're very welcome." While he wrote, for some reason her name was sounding familiar to him. When he realized why, he handed the signed napkin back with a grin. "You wouldn't be Congresswoman Georgia Fitzpatrick? Chair of the Natural Resources Committee?"

"Why, yes, I am," she replied, clearly flattered that he knew who she was. Smiling down at Morgan, she offered a hand draped in a tasteful combination of gold and diamonds. "I recognize you from your picture on the Mustang Ridge Conservancy's website. It's a pleasure to meet you, Ms. Whittaker."

"And you, too. Would you two like to join us for dessert?"

Brilliant, Ty thought as the friendly couple quickly agreed. Just as she'd done with Craig, Morgan had landed on the best way to make her case: by dazzling her audience. Once the waiter had brought them all coffee, their chance encounter quickly moved from pleasantries to what had brought them across the country in the first place.

"More of our wild places are disappearing every day," the congresswoman lamented, getting a grim nod from her husband. "It's heartening to discover that there are young people dedicated to preserving them for future generations."

"My family's been in Mustang Ridge since

1882, before Montana was a state," Morgan told her in an honest, straightforward manner that was clearly charming their unforeseen guests. "I want my daughters to grow up country girls like I did, hiking up in the Bridger Mountains, riding their ponies out on the prairie. I recognize that we need to hunt for new sources of energy, but the likelihood of finding anything in our area is remote, at best. I'm not sure why Cartwright Energy is even bothering with us."

Georgia traded a long look with her husband, who frowned into his half-empty coffee cup. Obviously choosing his words carefully, he said, "I'm on the legal counsel team for a lawsuit against, among others, Cartwright Energy. While I can't comment on that specifically, I can tell you that they've earned a reputation for digging first and analyzing later."

"Why?" Ty asked, baffled by the nonsensical approach.

"That's an excellent question, son, and one we're trying to answer without much success. But we'll keep at it until we have."

Grinning, Ty did something he once thought he'd never do. Toasted a lawyer. "To stubbornness and good sense."

They clanked their cups while the women looked on, smiling at them as if they were lunatics.

After a few more pleasant minutes, Neil stood and held out an arm for his wife. "Thank you for indulging us. We'll leave you to enjoy your desserts in peace."

"I'm looking forward to seeing you both tomorrow," Georgia said, beaming at each of them in turn before walking away with her husband.

"That was kinda cool," Ty announced.

"Yeah, now that I know someone on the committee besides Craig, the job feels a little less intimidating."

She was still nervous, though. While she was as determined as ever to make the most of the opportunity, her voice had an uncertain thread running through it. Hoping to ease her mind, he said, "You don't just know someone. You know the head honcho. That's gonna help a lot."

"I hope so."

Ty was hunting for a way to lift her spirits when the waiter came over and offered them a long silver tray of bite-size desserts. Ty was pretty well stuffed, but as Morgan's face lit up in anticipation, he decided it wouldn't kill him to try a few.

"Just leave it," he suggested with a grin. The server smiled back and set the tray in the center of the table before leaving them to their treats.

"These are awesome," Ty announced, pointing to the tiny layer cake covered in pale green frosting.

"They all are," she said, leaning back with a sigh. "I've never had a meal like this anywhere. It was really nice of Craig to arrange it for us."

"Yeah, he's a great guy."

Morgan eyed him curiously. "Why am I getting the feeling you don't really mean that?"

He shrugged, but she kept staring at him until he wanted to squirm. "Okay, fine. When he came out to Mustang Ridge, it was pretty easy to see that he liked you."

"That's good, because I wanted him to."

"Yeah, that was obvious." Ty heard the envy in his voice, and it made him cringe. Craig's comment that day about there being something between Ty and Morgan popped up in his memory, and he did his best to shrug it off. Morgan could flirt with any guy she chose, date him if she wanted to. It was none of his business. Feeling like an idiot, he tried to cover his tracks. "You two should get together while we're here."

"We are." Ty couldn't help grimacing, and for some crazy reason, she smiled. "Ty, are you jealous of Craig?"

"Course not." She leveled a give-me-a-break look at him, and he circled his neck to loosen the muscles that had knotted up during their uncomfortable exchange. "All right, maybe a little. He's smart and smooth, and he probably knows how to do his own tie."

Shaking her head, she laughed. "Moron. I meant Craig and I will see each other at the presentation tomorrow. I'm not interested in him romantically. I wanted him to like me so he'd pay more attention to the conservancy and what we're trying to accomplish. You know, that old saying about catching more flies with honey?"

"So, it wasn't flirting but strategy. Well, now—that's a horse of a different color."

She studied him across the table for long enough that he started to get that squirmy feeling again. When she finally spoke, he braced himself for a good shot.

Instead, very quietly she asked, "Why do you even care?"

It was an excellent question, and one he

didn't currently have a decent answer for. He searched for a humorous comeback but came up empty. So he went with the truth. "I'm not sure. I just do."

The corner of her mouth quirked into a very feminine smirk. "That's kind of flattering."

Ty let out a relieved sigh and managed to chuckle at his own foolishness. "That's good, 'cause from where I'm sitting, it sounded pretty lame."

"As an explanation, it was. But I appreciate you being honest with me."

Something between them had changed since she'd forgiven him. While he couldn't begin to identify what it might be, his gut was telling him to take advantage of some precious time alone with Morgan. Standing, he pulled out her chair for her. "I've never been to Washington. How 'bout you?"

"This is my first visit."

Offering his arm to her, he grinned. "Then let's go have ourselves an adventure. Whattya say?"

After a moment, the feistiest, most maddening woman he'd ever known stood and took his arm. "I say let's go."

Outside, he noticed that a large section of pavement had been blocked off in paint.

Looking farther down the street, he saw what must have been there earlier and just couldn't help himself.

Looking down at Morgan, he asked, "Wanna take a carriage ride?"

"Seriously? Did you look at the prices?"

"I saved a nice chunk of change on dinner, so I can swing it. Come on—it'll be fun. Long as you don't mind letting someone else handle the horses you're riding behind."

"So funny," she retorted, but let him tug her toward the platform beside a dainty copper-colored mare and a shiny black carriage. Typical cowgirl, she stepped up to the horse and offered a hand for her to sniff. "Hey there, pretty girl. What's your name?"

"Cecilia," the driver answered, touching the tip of his top hat in a quaint gesture that matched his vintage suit. "And I'm Tom."

"Gorgeous mare," Ty said. "What kind is she?"

The driver beamed as if Ty had just complimented him on one of his children. "She's a purebred Morgan, born and raised on my family's farm in Maryland."

Ty grinned at the odd coincidence of the horse's breed matching Morgan's name. "Well, that settles it. This is the one for us. We've never been to Washington, so how long does it take to see everything on your route?"

"An hour." After Ty handed over the money to cover it, he helped Morgan into the plush seat and then climbed up after her. Once they were settled, Tom prompted his horse with a simple "Let's go, Cecilia," and they were off.

The carriage moved at a much slower pace than the tour buses that were still darting from one sight to another, which gave them time to enjoy the balmy summer evening. Unlike the other tourists, they were treated to the sounds of a jazz band playing in a small park, and the scent of cinnamon-sugar-coated pecans wafting from a vendor's cart on the sidewalk.

"This was a meeting place for the government in the early days," Tom told them, pointing out an unassuming building in a row of other Federal-style structures. "They didn't have a name for it back then, but these days, we call it the Patriot. The man who owned it was part of George Washington's spy ring. His wife used to send coded messages to the passing American troops by how she hung her laundry out on washday."

"You're kidding," Ty commented, suspecting it was just some local folklore intended to charm the visitors.

"I've read about Washington's spies," Morgan said. "Without them, we never would've won the Revolutionary War."

"It's true," Tom agreed. "Brilliant military tactics and determination weren't enough to get the job done when we were outnumbered and outgunned. It just goes to show what regular people can accomplish when they all pull together for the same cause."

"True enough," Ty acknowledged, grinning over at Morgan. "I think there's a message for us in there, too."

"I think you're right. Thanks for suggesting we do this," she added with a smile. "It's the perfect way to unwind after a long day."

Resting her head on his shoulder, she let out a contented sigh that let him know she'd finally relaxed. Being cozied up in a carriage with her wasn't something he could have anticipated, but now that they were here, he couldn't imagine any place he'd rather be. Stretching his arm along the back of the low seat, he dropped a kiss on top of her head. "Anytime."

It had been an impulsive thing to do, and he half expected her to pull away from him to the opposite end of the seat. To his relief, she cuddled against him in a way he'd once thought he'd never experience again with her.

So, while Tom continued their entertaining and informative tour, Ty settled back to enjoy himself. In the warm evening air, he drank in the sensation of being with the only woman he'd ever met who could melt his heart with one look and cut him off at the knees with the next.

A romantic carriage ride through the historic district of Washington hadn't been part of the plan when he'd agreed to accompany Morgan on this trip. But it was the kind of surprise he could definitely live with.

Morgan had taken on plenty of challenges in her life.

She'd fallen off horses at a gallop, whipped around barrels at an angle that left her head dangling within inches of the hard metal. She'd even run off a full-grown cougar that had been eyeing a newborn mustang, sizing it up for his next meal. And when Allie had been diagnosed with autism, she'd fought to make sure her daughter got every last scrap of help she could find.

But nothing had prepared her for staring down a panel of immaculately dressed politicians who were politely sitting in their chairs, waiting for her to speak.

There were more than she'd anticipated,

each sitting in front of a sign that listed their name and which state they represented. From Colorado, Utah and Wyoming, all the way to Alaska, they were from places that had a keen interest in responsibly developing the natural resources that lay under America's soil. She knew that their shared concern for the environment should have made her feel more comfortable approaching them. But it didn't.

She'd practiced this speech in front of Ty and her family many times, but at this moment she couldn't recall how she'd decided to begin her presentation. She wasn't allowed to stand or move around, because she had to stay behind the microphone on the table in front of her so everyone could hear her. Her siblings called her Morgan the Brave, and she was glad they weren't here to see this. She was fairly certain she was an unflattering shade of green, and she'd rather keep this bout of queasiness to herself.

Beside her, cool as ever, sat Ty, who was eyeing her with a sympathetic expression. Covering the mike, he leaned in and murmured, "They wanna hear what you have to say, Morgan. Show 'em why Mustang Ridge is worth saving."

Mustang Ridge is worth saving.

His last words echoed in her mind, tripping

some kind of switch that calmed her jangling nerves enough for her to think. And then, like a bolt of friendly lightning, her opening appeared in her mind, and she silently thanked God for the assist.

"Hello, my name is Morgan Whittaker, and I've come here from Mustang Ridge, Montana. It's a picturesque small town near the Bridger Mountains, and my family has been there since 1882, before Montana was even a state."

A quick glance at Georgia showed her that the chair recognized the line from last night, and she got a quick nod of approval. "Generations of families have raised their children there, and I'm no exception." Taking out a large photo of the girls, she turned it for them to see and smiled. "These are my little cowgirls, Allie and Hannah. I want them and their friends to be able to grow up in the same beautiful, unspoiled place I did."

"They're adorable," one of the men commented, giving her a grandfatherly smile. "How old are they?"

She recognized that he was trying to put her at ease, and she thanked him with a smile of her own. "Six. They're twins."

There were murmurs of admiration, and then Georgia motioned for her to continue.

"And these," Morgan went on, taking up the next photo, a long panoramic shot of the mustangs coming through their valley at a dead run, "are descendants of the original herds that gave our town its name. The Mustang Ridge Conservancy is a group of citizen volunteers determined to protect them and the area around us from energy companies that have a tendency to dig first and analyze later."

She'd borrowed the phrase from Neil Fitzpatrick, and again Georgia nodded slightly. Morgan's pitch wasn't overly long, since her audience of guinea pigs had suggested it was best to keep it simple and leave ample time for questions. When she was finished, she held her hands out in the open-minded gesture Jessic had recommended. "If you have questions, I'll be happy to try to answer them."

"I have one," Craig Barlowe responded, then added his name as if they hadn't met before. Morgan considered that silly theatrics, but he was the expert, so she'd gone along with the ruse when he proposed it. "Is that the rodeo champion Ty Wilkins sitting next to you?"

"Yes, sir," Ty replied smoothly, leaning forward on his elbows in a casual pose to speak into the microphone. "Mustang Ridge is my hometown, and I'm proud to help out this worthy cause however I can."

His short, direct comment unleashed a ripple of hushed side conversations, and she was amazed by the effect his presence had on the committee members. Grudgingly, she had to admit that Craig had been dead-on about including Ty in their efforts here, and she pushed the mike toward him in a silent bid to take over.

"That being said," he went on, nudging the mike back, "I'm just a foot soldier in this fight. Morgan's built the conservancy from the ground up, and she's our general. She's the one you need to hear from."

Craig smothered a grin, but not before she noticed it. They'd set this up without telling her, she realized, and it had worked perfectly. These were the kind of folks who loved a good rodeo, and they clearly knew Ty, at least by reputation. But he'd come up with a tactic for handing off their questions to her, endorsing her without overshadowing her.

Rodeo star Tyler Wilkins had never been one to step away from the spotlight and let someone else shine in his place. But the man he'd become had done just that, and she made a mental note to thank him later. After she recovered from her impending nervous break-down, anyway.

She didn't know how long she fielded questions, and she lost track of how many there were. Most of them were pertinent, while others seemed to be a way to show interest without making a commitment to support their petition to gain governmental protection for the vast expanse of land identified on the latest survey of Mustang Ridge. The mapping had cost a small fortune, but as they passed it along the row to study, several people's reactions told her that the money had been well spent.

"This river," the representative from Alaska said, "does it serve the local area?"

"That's the Calico River, and yes, it does. Farms and ranches, along with wildlife that comes down into the foothills where they can find food and water to get them through the winter."

His eyes lit up enthusiastically. "What kind of wildlife?"

"Fish in the river, of course. Also cougars, wolves, deer, elk…" She rattled off every species she could think of, down to a colony of prairie dogs that had taken up residence there several years ago.

"Ms. Whittaker," he said in a calm tone that

had a thread of excitement running through it, "this isn't merely a matter of land rights. With so many animals freely roaming in and out of the area, Mustang Ridge sounds like a naturally occurring wildlife refuge."

Stunned by the revelation that should have been obvious to her before, Morgan fought to come up with a good response. Thankfully, Ty was quicker on his feet.

"Yes, it is," he said confidently. "It's great to know that someone else sees that, too."

Sitting back in his chair, the Alaskan folded his hands with a thoughtful expression. Morgan had no clue what he might be thinking, but at least her argument had made a tangible impact on someone other than Craig and Georgia. Quite honestly, she'd begun wondering if she'd have to invite them all to visit the way Craig had done, and show them what she was fighting so hard to protect. It hadn't occurred to her that their plight would resonate with people from faraway places who were waging the same battles.

Sad as it was to know other regions were struggling with the same problems, it was also comforting to know that not only did their elected officials understand, but they could help. All along, she'd instinctively known that the conservancy was too small to succeed without some heavy hitters on their side. Brooke Hamilton was a devoted member of the team, but even her legal expertise would only go as far as asking a judge to grant them a temporary reprieve from Cartwright's prospecting.

Who could have predicted that in the end it would be the animals that would make the difference?

Chapter Nine

It was a bright Monday morning in early August, and Morgan was just putting the finishing touches on the girls' smiley face pancakes. Between work and the never-ending demands of the conservancy she'd so impulsively started, she seldom got a day completely off. But Allie and Hannah would be headed back to school soon, and she was making a concerted effort to spend as much time with them as she possibly could. Kids were only young once, she reminded herself while she set the pancakes on two plates and drizzled syrup over them. You had to make the most of every phase they went through, because you didn't get a do-over on childhood.

"Here you go, ladies," she announced, delivering her load with a flourish. "Bon appétit."

"Where are yours, Mommy?" Hannah asked, her forehead wrinkling in concern. "I thought you liked them, too."

"I ate earlier, while I was catching up on some paperwork." Actually, she hadn't gotten much food down because the bank's annual accounting of their finances had soured her stomach. Running a profitable ranch these days was almost impossible unless you had a secret gold mine on the property somewhere. That thought led her to the latest salvo from Cartwright Energy informing the mayor that their impending exploration would begin in October, and her spirits sank even more.

To combat that, she refocused her worried mind on the reason she was doing all this in the first place: her girls. They might decide to move away to a big city someday, but she hoped they'd always remember their upbringing in this quiet, beautiful place. And that when they were mothers themselves, they'd be able to bring their children back to the same Mustang Ridge they'd grown up in.

"So, what should we do today?" she asked to get her mind off of the murky future of her hometown.

"Riding lessons," Allie suggested, surprising Morgan by being the first to respond. She normally let Hannah take the lead and then followed along. Come to think of it, Morgan had noticed the same tendency a few times recently, which was encouraging. She wished she knew what was enticing her timid girl to be more confident, so she could make sure to keep it coming.

"That would be fun," Hannah agreed, directing her comment to her twin. "And then we should go see the mustangs before it gets too hot. Maybe there are some new foals for us to name."

"If there are, I can draw them."

"That's a plan," Morgan announced, pleased that her daughters loved the wild herd as much as she did. It was a joy to share her love of wild things with them, and she hoped it would continue for a long time.

Then, out of nowhere, came a bellow from her father's den. "Laura!"

What followed was a muttered string of words that were mostly unintelligible, but the girls' matching blue eyes widened in astonishment. Dad wasn't prone to outbursts like this, and she could only imagine what had brought on this one.

"Why is Grandpa yelling at Grandma?" Hannah asked in confusion.

"No clue," Morgan replied as she got to her feet. "I'll go find out while you two finish your breakfast."

Hurrying down the hallway, she paused in the open doorway of the rustic study to take stock before entering his very masculine domain. Matilda, who was the unofficial queen of the house, was perched on top of a high bookcase, ears flattened while her raccoonish tail twitched in a show of feline temper. Dad sat slumped in his desk chair, chin in hand while he stared morosely at something on the computer. He was by nature an upbeat, positive man, and the defeated pose just about broke her heart.

"Dad?"

He didn't move, but his eyes flicked up to glance over at her. "Hmm?"

"Is everything okay in here?"

In answer, he waved his free hand at the monitor. Taking that as an invitation to come in, she crossed the room and leaned over to see what had set him off. He'd left an email open, and when she saw her mother's name in the From line, it made her stomach turn. The message was short and impersonal, which suggested to her that someone had helped write it.

Dear James,

This is a difficult letter for me to write, but I feel it needs to be done. Our separation has given me the chance to examine my life and what I want. My art career is going well, and I believe that it will succeed best in the more urban setting Helena has to offer. I will always care for you, but now that the children are all grown, the time has come for me to do what's best for me. I don't want any form of spousal support or any material objects from the house, only the freedom to live my life as I see fit. My decision is final, and I ask you to please sign and return these papers to my attorney as soon as possible.

Laura

Attached to it was a file ominously labeled Petition for Divorce. Morgan's own temper instantly began simmering, and she took a deep breath to settle it before speaking. Turning to her father, she sat on his desk, purposefully blocking the monitor from his view. "From your reaction, I'm assuming this isn't what you want."

"Of course not," he spat, jumping to his feet to begin an agitated pacing. "I agreed to the separation because I wanted her to get this craziness out of her system and come back to her family."

"Why? If she doesn't want to be here, that's up to her. We're doing fine without her."

"But she belongs here. She made a promise to me, to you kids. She should be here with us."

"Dad, I know it hurts, but I can't help thinking this is for the best." She went over to stand with him so he wouldn't feel so alone. "You're a great guy, and you deserve to be happy, instead of wasting time waiting around for someone who's never coming home."

He took a few seconds to absorb that, then slowly nodded, as if it pained him to do it. "Thanks for saying that, honey. In my head, I know you're right. But my heart isn't ready to let her go yet."

It had taken her months to get over losing Ty, so Morgan understood what he meant. Thinking back to her own situation, she vividly recalled what had hurt above anything. More than the humiliation, more than the missing him, she'd been cheated out of something that could have enabled her to move on a lot sooner. "Would it help if you could talk to her?"

"I think this—" he motioned to the computer "—is how she wants to do it."

"Too bad," Morgan seethed. "You were married for thirty years, and you have a right to settle this face-to-face. Not in some coward's-way-out email."

Once her furious words sank in, a slight grin brightened his stony features. "You noticed that, too? I think her lawyer wrote it for her."

"She owes you an explanation, in her own words, in person," Morgan declared, feeling more certain of that with each passing moment. "Helena's a couple hours away, and the address is at the bottom of her message. Go talk to her. Even if the end result is the same, at least you'll know you had a chance to have your say."

He gave her a knowing look. "Unlike you and Ty?"

"Well, yeah. Although I probably would've punched him besides. Considering you've got a bad shoulder, I wouldn't recommend that."

As she'd intended, he laughed and seemed to pull up a little straighter. She was glad to be able to help him that way, and she reached her arms around his waist for a hug. Leaning her head back, she smiled up at him. "No matter what happens between you and Mom, it's gonna be okay. I promise."

"I know." Returning the hug, he raked a hand through his thinning hair. "What I don't know is if I can confront her like you're suggesting. We haven't spoken to each other in over a year, and this isn't gonna be an easy conversation to start. Assuming she lets me in at all."

Morgan hated the uneasiness she heard in his voice, and without hesitation she said, "I'll go with you. I'll get the ball rolling and then leave you two alone. Do you think that might help?"

That earned her one of his trademark scowls. "I'm a grown man. I can manage this just fine on my own."

"You're also a big teddy bear, and you always back down when Mom puts up a fuss," she reminded him sternly. "My job will be to make sure you don't let her off the hook too easily. She's put you through a lot, and she should have to tell you to your face why she's doing this. You're entitled to that, and once you have it, you'll feel better about what's happened. Eventually," she added with an encouraging smile.

He thought it over, then nodded. "All right, let's get going before I change my mind."

"Ryan and Ben are out on the back section, but I'll call one of them to watch the girls. As soon as one of them is here, we'll leave."

It sounded like a great plan, until her call bounced back to her. She tried again, same result. They must be on the other side of the foothills, she realized with a frown. The cell service was nonexistent out there, and she could keep calling all morning and never reach them. She hated to leave her father to his difficult errand without backup, but there didn't seem to be any choice.

When he joined her in the front hallway, she didn't waste time sugarcoating the situation. "Dad, the boys are out of cell range, so I can't reach them. I won't be able to go with you, after all. I'm sorry."

His usually cheerful expression dimmed, but he quickly recovered, masking his disappointment with a smile. "That's all right. It's a long drive, anyway."

"You can still go," she insisted, willing him to agree for his own sake. "You should talk to Mom so you can put an ending on this and get on with your life."

"It's already over, so what's the point? I don't really have anything to say. I'll just sign those forms and mail them to her lawyer like she asked."

Stubborn to the bone, it wasn't like him to give up on anything. Then she understood what was going on. "You're afraid of what she'll say, aren't you?"

"Course not," he snorted, a spark of her own temper glittering in his eyes. After a moment, though, his manner softened, and he sighed. "Maybe. Sometimes I wonder if there's something I could've done to make things better. She never seemed unhappy here, so I didn't know there was anything wrong until she left."

Morgan knew how that felt, getting broadsided by someone you trusted, wondering what on earth had gone wrong. The difference for her was that Ty had found the courage to 'fess up and admit that what had driven him away wasn't her fault, but his. Her father deserved that same peace of mind, and she wanted him to have it.

"Why don't we just wait until tomorrow?" she suggested. "I can arrange for someone to watch the girls, and we'll go then."

"Or," Dad countered with a thoughtful look, "we could ask Ty."

"Seriously?"

"Why not? I saw him around earlier, so he's

not working at the feed store today. He loves the girls, and it's only for a few hours. Then I can get this outta the way before it drives me crazy."

He had a point, Morgan acknowledged. Their industrious neighbor had been outside his small ranch house all morning, doing handyman types of jobs on the exterior. It wasn't as if he had nothing to do, but home repairs could wait. Beyond that, she knew that he'd jump at the chance to help her dad while spending time with Allie and Hannah. It was a win, all the way around.

It couldn't hurt to ask, she decided while she pulled up his number. If he was willing to help out, their tense mission would be over by this afternoon. If not, they'd go tomorrow.

"Hey there, cowgirl," he answered on the second ring. "What's up?"

As much as his overly familiar attitude toward her had bothered her when he first showed up, she had to admit that she was beginning to like hearing his customary greeting again. Casual, but affectionate, it made her think that they just might be on their way to being friends.

After she'd laid out the reason for her call, he didn't hesitate. "Gimme five minutes to clean up, and I'll be right over. If JD's ready to make that trip, we don't want him putting it off and changing his mind."

"Thanks, Ty. I really appreciate it." Not only for his help, she realized. But his instinctive way of agreeing that her father needed to end his marriage on his terms, not those of a selfish woman who couldn't even be bothered to pick up a phone.

"Anytime, MJ. You know that."

She did once, she thought as she ended the call. But it was a nice sentiment, and she was grateful for the gesture. It almost made up for the fact that he'd once again called her MJ. When would he stop doing that?

By the time she'd filled in the girls on their change of plans, Ty was knocking on the front door.

"Have a good trip, Mommy," Allie said, adding a light hug before returning to her artwork.

"We'll feed Skye and Matilda for you," Hannah added helpfully.

"Thanks, honey, that's a big help."

It struck her that neither of them had asked about their absent grandmother. She felt a pang of sorrow that her mother had been gone so long, they didn't miss her. Laura Whittaker had lost something precious when she abandoned her family to set out on her grand adventure. Morgan hoped she was happy with her choice, because it had cost her an awful lot.

Ty wouldn't have been her first option as a babysitter. Although he'd abided by her conditions for seeing their daughters, she wasn't entirely comfortable with him being in charge of them for so long. But he waited patiently while she ran down a list of dos and don'ts, and she had to give him credit for humoring her.

While he walked them out to the truck, she continued her instructions. "I promised them a riding lesson, and I don't mind if you do that. They have to wear their riding helmets, and they only ride Belle, the gray Shetland. They're good for their age, but they're not ready for anyone taller. If they want to see the mustangs, drive them out there. It's too long a ride for them at their age."

"Got it."

Dad was already in the driver's seat of his SUV, and he spread his hands in a frustrated gesture that spoke for itself. Morgan got in beside him, and Ty closed the door behind her.

"Don't worry," he said with a reassuring smile. "I'll take good care of the girls while you're gone. You can count on me."

"Okay."

It didn't feel okay, though, and she cork-screwed in her seat to stare back at the house. He waved, then went back inside.

"Try not to worry so much," her father advised in a soothing tone. "After all, you're leaving Allie and Hannah with their father."

Yeah, Morgan thought apprehensively. That was the problem, although she couldn't deny that he'd gone to a lot of trouble to prove himself to her. The reckless young man who'd broken her heart all those years ago certainly hadn't been father material, and she stood by her decision to cut him out of the girls' lives.

But now, she wasn't so sure. He seemed more settled these days, and he'd followed her suggestions about rehabbing his house into an open, family-friendly place. She seldom had time to mull things over this way, but as the miles flew by, she began to wonder: Was it possible that Ty wanted to be more than a part-time father?

The concept wasn't as far-fetched as it might have seemed to her a few weeks ago. The trouble was, if they were meant to be together, it probably would have happened by now. But *probably* wasn't *definitely*, her heart reminded her. Another strong voice chimed in to remind her that letting her emotions take the lead had gotten her into trouble with the charming cowboy in the first place. Being practical had kept her on solid footing for most of her life, and it was the path she normally chose because it just made sense.

But things between Ty and her had rarely made sense, she acknowledged with a quiet sigh. Because when you loved someone, no matter how foolish it was, you couldn't help yourself. Not that she felt that strongly about him anymore, of course. That ship had sailed long ago, and she had no intention of taking another voyage through all that craziness.

Still, she had to admit—at least to herself—that loving Ty Wilkins was a very hard habit to break.

"Heels down, Allie," Ty reminded her, jiggling the long line to keep Belle at a pony's version of a jog. "Grip with your legs a little more and follow how she's moving." After she made the adjustment, he added, "That's it. Looking good."

The girl nodded and looked down at her hands, which were cemented in the low position he'd instructed her to use.

Quiet hands, he heard his grandfather saying in his memory. *Horses are smart, so stay out of his way and you'll do fine.*

Thoughts of the old wrangler brought Ty both a smile and a tinge of sadness. He lived in a nursing home in Helena now, his world constrained by the Alzheimer's that was slowly taking him away. During their last visit, he'd seemed content in his bright, sunny room, but had no idea who Ty was. When he introduced himself, Grandpa nodded absently and began talking about his grandson, a twenty-year-old who was a bright new star on the rodeo circuit.

Nine years gone, just like that. Ty's heart still twisted in sorrow, but knowing that he existed in his grandfather's memory somewhere made the changes a little easier to take.

Returning his attention to his eager student, he guided Allie through making a wide circle to change directions in the ring. She was a natural, he mused proudly, watching the small balancing adjustments she made without any prompting from him. Her affinity for animals, both large and small, was a real talent. With the right schooling and encouragement, that skill could land her a fulfilling job when she was older. In the meantime, she was getting a great education here on the ranch, and he silently thanked God for sending her to a family that would take such good care of her.

"And stop in the middle," he said. Once the horse was still, he reeled in the lunge line as he strolled to the center of the ring. Hannah had appreciated a hug at the end of her lesson, but he cautioned himself to keep his distance from Allie. Running a hand along the pony's neck, he smiled at the shy child. "You did a real nice job with her. I think she enjoyed herself. How 'bout you?"

After a moment, she offered up a shy smile and nodded. "It was fun."

He didn't usually get a gesture and verbal response from her at the same time, and it was all he could do to resist pulling her into a warm embrace. Instead, he gave himself a mental high five for making progress with her. "I'm glad to hear that. Why don't you hop down, and we'll go rub down Belle before we turn her out with her buddies in the pasture?"

"Okay."

She dismounted smoothly, and from her seat on the top rail, Hannah asked, "Ty, can I have a ride?"

"It's almost lunchtime, so I think we're done for now."

"No," she replied, laughing as if he'd just suggested they fly to the moon for a picnic. "A piggyback ride. That's what Mommy does after a lesson."

He didn't doubt that for a second, he mused with admiration. "Well, if that's the routine, I guess we better stick to it."

He angled over to pick up his passenger, who clambered onto his back and held on tight. Feeling like a good dad, he headed for the front barn with the pony on one side of him and Allie on the other. Sometimes, he still couldn't quite believe that he had daughters, much less ones as awesome as these two. He'd had a wild, exciting life out on the circuit, but these days there was nothing he liked more than hanging out with his little cowgirls.

When he felt a small hand slide into his, he glanced down at Allie, and the half smile she gave him would have melted an entire Alaskan glacier. Ty's heart swelled with pride, knowing that, in spite of his many flaws, he'd stumbled on a way to connect with this special child. Their shared love of animals was the key, he recognized. Well, that and a whole lot of patience. And then it hit him.

It hadn't been all that hard. Was it possible that he was meant to be in their lives all along, and God had ended his rodeo career to bring him home to the children who needed him to be their daddy? It wasn't much of a leap for him to make, and he toyed with the idea until they got to the barn and the twins began untacking their lesson partner.

"You two make a great team," he approved, arms crossed while Allie removed the saddle and Hannah the bridle. Together, they lifted the heavy saddle pad, flipping it before draping it over the saddle on its rack. Ty recognized the careful handling as Morgan's, who at ten years old had been the one to scold him for just dropping his tack on the floor after a ride.

"If you take care of things right, you'll have them for a long time," Hannah informed him in a voice that echoed her mother's, only at a higher pitch.

"That's true," he agreed, handing them each a curry brush while he grabbed a comb to start on the pony's mane. "And not just about things, but people, too."

"You sound like Grandpa," she told him.

Pausing in his work, he smiled over at her. "That's just about the nicest thing anyone's ever said to me, honey. Thanks."

"He's a good grandpa," Allie commented, patting Belle's shoulder while she worked.

"I have a good one, too. His name is Vernon."

"What's he like?" Hannah asked.

And so, Ty described the wise man who'd

taught him so much about life, leaving out the sadder parts to avoid upsetting them. When it seemed like he'd rambled on long enough, he finished up with, "He's a great guy, and I love him a lot."

For some reason, his comment got Allie's attention, and she gazed at him with the thoughtful expression he'd noticed on her many times. Nothing could have prepared him for what she said.

"You'd be a good daddy."

Ty's brain seized completely, and he couldn't come up with a single thing to say. As they stared at him like cute blond bookends, he rallied and finally said, "That'd be cool someday."

"We don't have a daddy," Hannah said in a matter-of-fact way that drove a spike into his heart. After a pause, she looked up at him and went on. "Would you like to be ours?"

Yes! Ty wanted to blurt, but logic broke in and stopped him. His promise to Morgan about keeping his true identity secret rang in his ears, and he knew if he broke it, she'd be furious. Would probably want to kill him, and he couldn't blame her. It had taken him two months to regain her trust enough that she let him have limited time alone with their daughters. He didn't want to do anything to jeopardize that.

But another part of him, one he didn't even know existed, responded to them on a different level that didn't know the first thing about being reasonable and cautious. It was the instinctive part of him that reacted to a panicky horse without thinking, and it was the one he followed now.

Strolling over to a nearby hay bale, he reminded himself that they were six and he needed to keep things simple and kid friendly. Then he sat down and patted the open spot on either side of him. "Come on over, girls. There's something I need to tell you."

"This is it," Dad announced, shifting the SUV into Park outside a double unit in a Helena condominium complex. The buildings looked new, and the grounds were expertly landscaped, with lots of mature trees and well-maintained gardens full of flowers. Each set was a duplex with a garage in front and a covered patio out back inside a small yard framed by shrubs that defined the property lines without being too obvious about it.

In short, it looked like a very pleasant place. As they left the truck and walked up the driveway toward the front door, the odd feeling Morgan had been experiencing all morning intensified with each step. This was her mother's new home, she thought grimly. The woman had been here for nearly a year, and none of them had ever seen this place. There was just something wrong about that.

This reunion was for her father's benefit, so she hung back while he went up on the small landing and rang the doorbell. For some reason, the cheerful summertime colors in the wreath hanging on the blue front door rubbed her the wrong way. It was as if she'd expected to find her mother living in a dismal studio apartment instead of this bright, vibrant place, and Morgan chided herself for being so foolish. Clearly, Mom was far from pining for the family she'd left behind. How that could be true baffled Morgan, but the evidence was right here in front of her eyes.

A slender figure showed up in one of the sidelights, blurred by the sheer curtain as it stared out at them in apparent disbelief. Out of respect for Dad, Morgan swallowed a less-than-gracious comment and tamped down her impatience for this unwelcome task to be over with already.

After what felt like an exceedingly long delay, the sound of a chain sliding reached them, and the door slowly swung inward.

She looked the same, Morgan noticed with more than a little surprise. Tall and willowy, her blond hair pulled back into a ponytail, a smudge of purple spotting her chin. The smell of paint wafted out to them, accompanied by strains of the soothing kind of music that Morgan assumed people listened to when they were doing yoga. That was new, she noted wryly. Apparently, Mom had made a few changes, after all.

"James," she said in a stunned voice. When her bright violet eyes fell on Morgan, there was a twinge of something in them. It might have been regret, but at this point, Morgan really didn't care. "Morgan. How nice of you to come by."

Come by? Was she kidding? She made it sound as if they'd been around the corner and stopped in on their way home. Morgan's simmering temper was threatening to boil over, and she struggled to keep it under control. This woman had walked out on her husband and children months ago, with no warning and no explanation, and now she was acting as if it had never happened. Morgan was smart enough to realize that her mother's disappearance mirrored Ty's, which was probably why it bothered her so much.

Loyalty was the number one priority for

her in any relationship, and they'd both betrayed her in the worst possible way. Then it occurred to her that Ty had begun to redeem himself in her eyes, and she'd finally forgiven him for hurting her so badly. Her mother was another story, but it wasn't her place to speak up now. This trip was about Dad getting on with his life, and if keeping her peace would help him accomplish that, she'd gladly do it.

But when they got home, she was taking a long ride into the Bridger foothills, where she could scream out her frustration in privacy, with only the coyotes and hawks to hear her.

"It's good to see you, Laura. You're looking well," Dad replied calmly, impressing Morgan with his control.

"I'm very happy," she told him in a clipped but polite tone. Motioning behind her, she added, "I'd invite you in, but I'm painting the foyer so it's a mess right now."

"Not a problem. We can talk out here just as well as anywhere."

"Talk?" she echoed, blinking at him as if she didn't understand the concept. "About what?"

Morgan seriously wanted to strangle her. Because she didn't trust herself to look at her mother without spitting, she directed her comment to her dad, who was clearly handling the situation better than she was. "You two should have some privacy. I think I'll wait in the truck."

"Thanks, honey," he said. "I won't be long."

She turned to go and then heard her name. Turning back, she forced herself to meet her mother's eyes directly. "Yes?"

"How are Allie and Hannah? Do they ever ask about me?"

"They're fine," Morgan answered politely. She could have left it there, but after all the kowtowing she'd done on behalf of the conservancy, she'd grown tired of being nice to people who didn't deserve it. "And no, they don't."

Having delivered the message that had been stuck in her craw for months, she turned and strode to the SUV without even a glance back. When she thought about this later, she might regret being so harsh with her mother, but she honestly didn't care.

She made a point of focusing on her phone to avoid watching the awkward scene unfolding on the front stoop. Every once in a while, she glanced up to make sure Dad was holding his own. She was pleased to find that he seemed to be doing most of the talking, while Mom sat there, hands folded in her lap, looking contrite.

Finally, he got to his feet and handed over the envelope that contained the forms he'd signed and brought with him. Mom stood and took them from him, clutching them to her chest while she thanked him. Then, after a brief embrace, Dad turned and headed for the truck.

As they drove away, Morgan checked the side mirror and found her mother standing in front of her pretty new home, watching them go. One of those full-circle moments, Morgan thought with a mixture of sadness and relief. At least this time it was Dad doing the leaving.

Hoping her father saw it that way, she kept her voice light. "So, how're you feeling?"

"Sad," he admitted with a grimace. "But I'm glad you insisted on me seeing her in person again. I got to say my piece, and now it's over. She doesn't want anything from me in the divorce except her freedom, so I gave it to her."

"I don't know why you made it so easy for her, bringing those papers with you," Morgan seethed. "I would've made her sweat, waiting for me to mail them back the slowest way possible."

He actually chuckled at that. "I know, but you're not me. When you get to be my age, you realize there's no shame in taking the high road. This way, it's over for both of us today. Now I can forgive her and move on."

"Forgive her?" Morgan echoed in disbelief. "Why? She certainly doesn't deserve it."

"Maybe not, but I do. Holding a grudge takes a lot of energy, and I've got no intention of letting this ruin any more of my life than it already has. Life is short, and to me, having peace of mind is priceless."

Reaching over to rub his shoulder, she said, "I'm sorry, Dad. Today must be really hard for you."

"I loved her for a long time, even after she left. Life doesn't always turn out the way we want it to, but we have to keep going and work with what we get." Looking over, he gave her a grateful smile. "I've got the best family a man could ask for. I thank God for the bunch of you every day."

"We thank Him for giving us you," she assured him, smiling back. She felt a lot better than she had just a few minutes ago. "You're the most amazing dad and grandpa ever."

"Thanks, honey. I really needed to hear that."

The wistfulness she heard was understandable, and she let him dwell on those feelings for a few minutes. Then, she decided it was time to lift his spirits. "I'm starving. How 'bout you?"

"Sounds good to me. Is there a diner around here somewhere?"

"Diner?" she scoffed, waggling her phone at him. "I found a good, old-fashioned steakhouse that serves bison and venison. Whattya say?"

Laughing, he signaled the turn that her GPS indicated he should take. "I say let's eat."

It was later that afternoon when JD's truck pulled into the turnaround in front of the house. Ty was on the front porch, where he'd been for the last hour, trying to figure out a way to tell Morgan what had happened during the day. He knew she'd be furious with him for reneging on their agreement, and he needed to find the right approach for coming clean.

Nothing had come to mind so far, so he was going to have to resort to the strategy he'd used when taking on an unfamiliar bull on the rodeo circuit. Wing it.

He was on his way down the steps to meet her when two blond whirlwinds flew past him and out to greet her. His chest seized in outright terror, but there was nothing he could do to stop what was already in motion. They crushed Morgan in a delighted hug, alternating turns to tell her about the fun day they'd had while she was gone. And then he heard Hannah say the words that spiked through the warm air like nails in his coffin.

"Mommy, Mommy! Ty is our daddy! Isn't that awesome?"

In a single instant, the joy on Morgan's face froze over, and she slowly lifted her gaze to stare at him. There was no emotion in those vivid blue eyes, which had gone as icy as her expression, and he actually gulped down a wave of abject fear. He would have much preferred anger or accusations over the nothing that he was getting from her right now.

Oh, yeah, he thought with genuine remorse. *This was going to get ugly.*

For his part, JD breezed past the awkward moment, shepherding the girls inside to leave Ty and Morgan alone. His boots felt like lead, but he forced himself to walk over and take his beating like a man.

Facing her squarely, he waited for her to start. When she just kept staring at him, he realized this might take a while. Finally, he couldn't take it anymore and attempted to get things moving with a little well-placed humor. "Ladies first."

"Not here," she shot back, stalking toward

the fence that separated his property from the Whittakers'. When they were a good distance from the house, she stopped and spun to face him. "We had an agreement, Tyler, one that you and I both promised we'd abide by. What happened?"

When she used his full name, it wasn't a good sign. But at least she was talking, and he appreciated her giving him a chance to explain instead of kicking him in the shins like when they were kids. So he nutshelled his conversation with Allie and Hannah before adding, "I guess I lost my head when they started talking about how much they'd enjoy having a dad of their own to do things with. I love those little girls, and you know I want to be their father for real."

"So this was my fault?"

"No, it's mine," he quickly corrected her, holding up his hands in surrender. "I'm just saying that what I did came from the heart, not any intention to hurt you or undermine your relationship with them."

She chewed on that for a few seconds, and he hoped that she might be coming around to his way of thinking. Unfortunately, he was wrong. Again.

"And Washington?" she spat, as if the word tasted bitter to her now. "Was that your sneaky way of loosening me up so I'd be more likely to go along with this little scheme of yours to weasel your way into my family?"

His patience was quickly wearing thin, but he took a breath to calm his voice before speaking. Considering the frame of mind she was in, one wrong word could shatter the fragile trust he'd been working so hard to build. "You know me better than that. I'd never do that to anyone, and especially not you."

Because I love you, he was tempted to add, then thought better of it. Not because it wasn't true, but because it wasn't the right time to tell her. She might view it as another attempt to manipulate her feelings, and then he'd be right back where he was the first day he showed up in Mustang Ridge. One thing was still the same, he realized morosely. She didn't trust him, and he was on his knees, begging for her forgiveness.

His mind raced for something else to say, to convince her that he'd meant no harm and just wanted the connection with his daughters that he'd been missing. But he acknowledged that there was nothing more he could do, so he waited for her to decide how she felt about him exposing their secret.

"Tell me something," she finally said in

an eerily calm tone that made his skin crawl. "Do you break a lot of your promises, or just the ones you make to me?"

Ty felt as if he'd gotten the wind knocked out of him, and he struggled to meet that cool glare evenly. "I don't give my word lightly, and when I do, I try my best to keep it."

"Could've fooled me."

Man, she's good, he thought, convinced that if he checked later on, he'd have welts from the sharp words she was flinging at him. Each one hit its mark, and he suddenly understood that she'd been waiting to lash out at him for a long, long time.

With that insight, he tried a different tack. "I deserve that." When he paused and she didn't argue with him, he took it as slight progress and forged ahead. "But I hope you'll believe that I never wanted to hurt you. When I left seven years ago, I honestly felt it was the best thing for both of us."

"And today?" He didn't answer right away, and she pounced like a ravenous cougar. "You'd do it again, wouldn't you?"

Suddenly tired of eggshell walking when it came to their daughters, he abandoned the apologetic route and took his own shot. "Yeah, I would. Maybe not the same way, but I'd want to tell them the truth about who

I am. I've been waiting for you to do that for weeks now, but you wouldn't. I guess I got tired of wondering when you'd finally decide it was the right time."

"I would've gotten there."

"When? At their high school graduation, when they were confused about why a guy who's just a friend of the family was so proud of them? At their weddings, when they needed someone to walk them down the aisle? When, MJ?"

She scowled at him, anger glittering in her eyes while she considered his question. And then, without warning, she spun on the heel of her boot and simply walked away.

Fine by him, he thought angrily as he turned and stalked in the other direction. The woman was all the handful she'd ever been, and more. With a sharp mind and a tongue to match, even on a good day she'd always had a knack for driving him straight to the edge of his sanity. Just because they were neighbors didn't mean they had to talk to each other. The pastures separating them were more than wide enough to give them both plenty of space.

But as he went past the riding ring where he'd given Allie and Hannah their lesson, he paused in his mental rant. Leaning on the rail, he could picture them on their patient pony, following his instructions and gaining in confidence with each circle. The breeze picked up a bit, and he took off his hat, dangling it over the fence while he stared at the ground.

Now that he'd had a chance to cool off, he was beginning to see things from Morgan's perspective. It occurred to him that, unlike his past mistakes, this one involved more than just the two of them. It affected innocent children who didn't deserve to be put in the middle of two people who couldn't manage to agree on much of anything. His ongoing problems with Morgan made him uncomfortably aware that they fought almost as much as his parents had, and if they were meant to be together, then it certainly would have happened by now.

So that was it, he realized as he put on his hat and picked up his heart from where it had fallen. Trudging toward home, he was forced to admit that he'd gone over the line with Morgan once again. Just when they'd managed to put the past aside and started building something new, he'd acted impulsively and destroyed it.

Apparently, he hadn't changed that much, after all.

Chapter Ten

"I'm sure we've done this one before," Jessie complained, flipping over the page she was filling out by hand.

"We did, but it disappeared into the legal system never to be seen again," Morgan told her. She heard the bitter edge on her voice but wasn't in the mood to do anything about it, so she willed her younger sister to let it go.

Fat chance.

"Morgan." When their eyes connected across the table, Jessie set down her pen and crossed her arms over the jumble of papers she'd been working on. "You've been out of sorts for days now. What's up?"

"There's just a lot going on. Sorry to be cranky."

"Is it Mom? I mean, Dad seems a lot happier now that the divorce paperwork is in process. He even asked Sharon Grainger to go to that auction with him today." Pausing, she laughed. "I can't believe she went, but it was cute how he changed his clothes three times before leaving."

"No, it's not that. I'm glad he's moving on, since that was the whole point of him going to see Mom in Helena."

Jessie gave her a long, suspicious look. "Then it's got to be Ty. I haven't seen him around here at all lately. What happened with you two?"

"Nothing." *That's the problem*, she added silently. Just when she'd started trusting him again, he'd gone and let her down in the worst way possible. Betraying her trust, getting their daughters excited about having their father in their lives. Whenever she thought about it, she could feel her blood pressure skyrocketing.

"Allie and Hannah keep asking when he's coming over, and you always put them off. That's not nothing. Now, spill it, or I'll keep guessing till I get it right. You know how annoying I can be," she added with a little-sister grin that would grate on the nerves of a saint.

"Fine. I'll tell you, but you have to promise to keep it to yourself."

"Deal. Now, 'fess up. You'll feel better if you tell someone."

Morgan laid it out for her, keeping her voice low to prevent it from traveling into the family room, where the girls were occupied playing the latest round of their favorite board game. When she was finished, she sat back and sighed. "So, that's what happened. Happy now?"

Jessie hesitated, as if she was trying to frame her response just right. That usually spelled trouble, and Morgan cautioned herself to be patient. It wasn't easy.

"You probably won't like what I have to say," Jessie finally began, toying with her pen to avoid looking up. "But I'm gonna say it anyhow." Lifting her eyes, she said, "I get where Ty's coming from. They're his daughters, too, and it's obvious he really loves them. He has a right to be part of the picture."

"He did," Morgan countered, "before he broke his promise to me. I'm their mom, and I get to decide who sees them and who doesn't."

"I know he agreed to your conditions, but it really wasn't fair of you to expect that to go on indefinitely. They're great kids, and he's proud to be their father. I know he hurt you terribly, but that was a long time ago. From what I've seen, he's done everything he can to mend fences with you."

"And then he broke them again," Morgan announced firmly. "That's his problem."

"And the girls," Jessie pointed out somberly. "They just found out that their father is the guy next door, and they're not allowed to see him. That's really sad."

Morgan was digesting that when a knock sounded on the back door. Brooke Hamilton, the conservancy's lawyer, stood on the porch, framed in the screen and smiling. Morgan had never been so glad to be interrupted in her life.

"Come on in, Brooke," she called out, waving her in. "We could use some good news right about now. I hope you've got some."

"Very good," the young attorney replied, sitting in an empty chair next to Jessie. Pulling a thin stack of papers from her briefcase, she beamed. "The judge granted our temporary stay. Cartwright Energy is blocked from doing any more prospecting in Mustang Ridge until all these conditions are met."

Fanning out the pages, she showed them the lengthy list of demands the conservancy had compiled. The judge had ticked most of them and crossed out a few others. But it was the front page that interested Morgan the most.

"'Cease and desist,'" she read with a surge of pride for what their little group of crusaders had accomplished. "My new favorite phrase."

"Mine, too," Brooke agreed enthusiastically. "When I was in law school, I dreamed about using what I was learning to really make a difference someday. Beating back a greedy corporation like this makes me feel like Robin Hood."

Standing, Morgan fetched three glasses from the dish drainer and took a pitcher of lemonade from the fridge. After filling the glasses, she raised hers. "To the Mustang Ridge Conservancy. May this be the first victory of many on our way to booting Cartwright Energy back over the Bridger Mountains where they belong."

While they toasted and drank to their success, her conversation with Jessie was still echoing in Morgan's mind. Thinking about Ty—and what had so nearly almost been— left her with a pang of regret.

He'd done so much to help make this happen, from lending his celebrity to the cause, to bringing Craig Barlowe in on the effort, to hours of helping her craft and hone her pitch to the committee in Washington. If things hadn't gone so far awry, Ty would have been here, celebrating with them.

But he wasn't. And she honestly couldn't envision how they might bridge the gap he'd created to find their way back to where they'd been during their DC trip. Normally, Morgan faced reality head-on and accepted situations for what they were.

This time, she just felt sad.

One morning, Perry rushed into the feed store as if he was being chased by an angry bull. "Ty, did you hear about the Connors place?"

"No," he replied, concerned by the urgency in his boss's tone. "What happened?"

"Frank and Sally have been trying to sell their extra acreage for years, but they could never find a buyer for their property. Kailani heard through the grapevine that Cartwright Energy made them an offer they couldn't refuse."

Morgan.

It had been two weeks since their last—and apparently final—blowup, but how she'd react to this news was the first thing that came into his mind. "The mustang herd crosses that spot to get to the river and up to their summer grazing on that swath of public land. Morgan has a permanent right of access for them to use it."

"Only as long as the Connors own it. If that changes—" Perry shrugged.

"There has to be a way to stop this." After a few seconds, he asked, "Did they sign the papers yet?"

"Not as far as I know."

"Can I take an early lunch?"

"It's eight in the morning," Perry argued, then grinned as the reason dawned on him. "You're gonna stop the sale, aren't you?"

"I'm sure gonna try."

"Anything I can do?"

"Not that I can think of. Thanks, though."

"No problem," Perry said, flipping up the hinged countertop to change places with Ty. "Call if you need me."

Ty waved in thanks as he all but ran from the store. On his way through town, he stopped in at the bank and emptied his savings of all but the few dollars required to keep the account open. It might not be close to the offer the couple had gotten already, he acknowledged as he raced along the road that led to their place. But it might be enough to stall until he could figure out something else.

Pulling up in front of the Connors' modest ranch-style home, he swung down from his truck and hurried up the front steps. Pulling in a few deep breaths, he summoned a friendly smile as he knocked on the screen door. It seemed to take forever, but finally Sally appeared in the hallway, squinting to see who was visiting so early. Fortunately, when she saw him, she beamed as if he was a long-lost son.

"Ty Wilkins," she greeted him, opening the door to let him inside. "It's so nice to see you."

Reminding himself to tread carefully, he accepted her welcoming hug. "It's nice to see you, too. I've been meaning to come by, and this morning seemed like the perfect time."

"How sweet. Come on in. I'll let Frank know you're here."

Sweet, he mused as he followed her into the sunny kitchen. Morgan had called him that a time or two, before he completely messed up and lost her for good. There was no help for that now, he reminded himself sternly. But the least he could do was make an attempt to save the mustangs she loved so much.

Taking a seat at the round table, he tried to organize what he wanted to say to the elderly couple, who had every right to sell their property to anyone they chose. He hadn't really thought about it, and suddenly it occurred to him that he didn't have a good reason for them to change their plans. When Frank appeared alongside his wife, Ty stood and shook the man's hand. "Good to see you, Mr. Connors. How've you been?"

The old farmer gave him a once-over and then, to Ty's surprise, he chuckled. "Well, news sure does travel fast in this little town."

"Don't be rude, Frank," his wife chided, pouring a cup of coffee and setting it in front of Ty. "This young man came all the way out here to see us. The least you can do is hear him out."

"I'm guessing you know why I'm here," Ty began, drinking some coffee to help his suddenly dry throat.

Frank sat back, folding his arms across his chest with a curious expression. "Morgan's been after us for months to buy that land. What I can't figure out is what you're doing in the middle of this? Word is she hasn't spoken to you in weeks."

Hearing it phrased like that smarted, but Ty put his own feelings aside and concentrated on his reason for being here. "I'm here to keep Cartwright Energy out of Mustang Ridge, for all our sakes. Once you give them a few acres, they'll use 'em as a foothold to buy up more land on either side. Before we know it, we'll all be living in an oil field."

"Their plans make a lotta sense to me," Frank countered. "They're pros, and they know what they're doing. If they do find oil here, we've been assured that they'll pump it without ruining the land around it."

"No one can promise that," Ty pointed out in the most controlled tone he could manage with his quickly panicking heart slamming away in his chest. Looking to Sally, he found a sympathetic face. "If they're wrong about the impact, they can just pull up stakes and leave. We're the ones who're gonna be left with the consequences."

Frank chewed on that for a few seconds, and Ty could tell the man was beginning to have second thoughts. Seizing on the opportunity, he pulled the bank envelope out of his rear pocket and set it on the table.

"What's this?" his host asked suspiciously. "A bribe?"

Forcing himself to sound casual, Ty replied, "A down payment. If you can stall Cartwright a few days, I'll get you the rest."

Interest flared in the man's eyes. "How much?"

Ty had no clue how much they'd accepted from the developer, so he sent up a quick prayer for help. After doing a quick mental inventory of his remaining possessions, he named a figure that thankfully didn't earn him a laugh. Instead, Frank stroked his chin pensively.

"That might be worth considering," he agreed, giving his wife a questioning look. "What do you think?"

She thought it over and then said, "I think we should have our lawyer check over that offer for us. That could take a week or so, with him being away on vacation and all."

Ty suspected their lawyer hadn't gone anywhere, and that she'd come up with a clever—and believable—way to hold off to give him the time he needed. Wary of getting too excited about something that could still fall apart, he asked, "Does that mean we have a deal?"

"If you can come up with what you're suggesting," Frank answered, "then yes, we have a deal."

He held out a calloused hand that had seen a lot of hard work over the years. It was a hand that Ty could respect, and he gladly shook it to seal their agreement.

"From one local boy to another," the farmer confided, "I wasn't too keen on selling to them, anyway."

"Keith and Trina weren't fans of the idea, either," Sally added. "They want to bring their kids here from California to visit in the fall."

"Oh, yeah?" Ty asked, leaning back to enjoy the rest of their visit. "Whereabouts do they live?"

"She and her husband live in Sacramento with their two boys, and Keith just moved there with his crew of three. He and his wife bought a beautiful new house, and he sent us some pictures. Would you like to see them?"

"Now, Sally," her husband said, "I'm sure Ty needs to get back to work."

"Perry's covering for me, so I'm good." He'd owe his old buddy big-time, but after the coup he'd just pulled off against the big, bad energy developers, he couldn't care less. "If you've got pictures, I've got plenty of time."

Friday afternoon, Morgan was on the front porch playing Go Fish with Allie and Hannah when a delivery truck pulled into the driveway and continued on to the house. The driver held a small folder-style envelope in his hand as he approached them and stopped at the base of the steps.

"Excuse me, ladies," he said pleasantly, touching the brim of his company's ball cap with a friendly smile. "I have a registered delivery for Morgan Whittaker. Is she around?"

"That would be me," she answered, setting her cards facedown on the table to meet him on the lawn. She noticed that the package had come from a bank in Helena, but she couldn't imagine what might be inside. It definitely was addressed to her, so she tipped the driver and gave him directions to his next stop a few miles down the road.

After he'd gone, she tamped down her curiosity long enough to lose four more hands of the game that Allie had an uncanny knack for. "You're turning into a real expert at this. What's your secret?"

"I ask you for the cards you asked me for earlier."

"That's really cool. How can you remember all those turns?" Hannah asked, clearly baffled by her twin's stunning memory.

"I just can."

That kind of laser focus was a feature of autism, Morgan knew. It was nice that among the many challenges Allie faced, there were some skills that came naturally to her. Morgan made a mental note to mention this development to Allie's teacher when school started. Hopefully, they could use it to hone her abili-

ties and help keep this special girl on the path
to a good, fulfilling life.

Once they were bored with beating her at
cards, she took them inside for a snack and
some art time. Summer vacation went by so
fast, and it was nearly September. She loved
her job, but there was nothing like spending
long, lazy days with her daughters, laughing and playing with them. Childhood came
around only once, and she'd gladly work until
midnight if it meant she could spend the afternoon with her girls.

While they munched and drew, she opened
the cardboard sleeve and set the contents on
the table. The pages were stapled onto an of-
ficial-looking backer, and at first she didn't
understand what she was looking at. There
was no letter of explanation, and a peek back
inside the sleeve showed her it didn't con-
tain one.

Interesting, she thought, turning her attention back to the document. It was a sales
agreement for some land in the area, and she
wondered if someone had donated it to the
conservancy anonymously, to keep folks from
discovering who they were. And then, she
saw the line that explained it all, and her heart
shot into her throat.

"Undeveloped tract of land referenced

herein is gifted to Morgan Jo Whittaker, in perpetuity, to use, preserve and protect for the remainder of her life, and thereafter, for the lives of her heirs."

Morgan was no lawyer, but she had enough knowledge of property grants to recognize that what she was holding in her hands was absolutely priceless. The location of the acreage in question registered with her immediately, and she took out her phone to call Ben.

"Yellow," he answered, punctuating his greeting with a grunt that told her he was still wrestling with the cranky antique baler out in the back hay field.

"How's it going?"

"Slow and hot. What's up?"

"I need you to come in and keep an eye on the girls for a little while," she explained. "I've got an errand to run, but I'll trade you the time after dinner tonight."

"Not a chance, sis. Between the ranch and the conservancy, you're doing enough already. I'm happy to get something to eat and hang out with Allie and Hannah till you come back."

Her youngest brother could be a royal pain in the neck when he wanted to be, but apparently this wasn't one of those times. "Thanks, Ben. I really appreciate it."

"No problem. I'll be there in ten."

He was true to his word, and after reminding her daughters to be good for him, Morgan got in her truck and headed for the Connors home. Like everyone else in town, she'd heard that they'd had an offer from Cartwright Energy, and she'd assumed they'd completed the sale to the developer. Finding out differently was an enormous surprise to her, and she wanted to thank them in person for helping to protect the unspoiled beauty of Mustang Ridge.

When she arrived, the two were in the middle of eating an early dinner. They graciously interrupted their meal and welcomed her inside.

"I'm sorry to disturb you," she said, "but I just got a very special delivery and wanted to thank you in person."

"For what, dear?" Sally asked, frowning in confusion.

When Morgan explained, Frank shook his head. "We sold the land to a private buyer, but we didn't deed it to you. That was his doing."

"Frank," his wife scolded in a whisper, slapping his arm with an oven mitt. "We were supposed to keep the details to ourselves. Remember?"

Looking chagrined, he clamped his mouth shut as if that would help the situation.

More confused than she'd been in a long time, Morgan glanced from one to the other, but neither of them said anything more. And then, in a flash of inspiration, it hit her.

Ty.

She didn't want to put the sweet couple in the position of confirming her suspicions, so she opted to drop the subject. "Well, however it happened, on behalf of the conservancy, I still want to thank you for deciding to keep the land in private hands. I promise you we'll use it for the benefit of everyone who lives here, whether they walk on two legs or four."

"Don't forget the snakes and the fish," Frank teased, obviously relieved to be let off the hook for blabbing.

"We won't," she promised, giving them each a grateful hug. "Once word of this gets around, I'm sure we'll be having a party to celebrate. If you don't mind, I'd like to include you on the guest list."

They agreed, and she bid them goodbye before heading back to her truck. While she drove away, her eyes went across the swale that separated the Connors' side yard from Ty's. She still didn't understand what was going on, and there was really only one way to find out. At the very least, she should call and thank him. He, more than anyone, knew that this piece of land was the buffer zone between possible development and the mustang herd she'd fought so hard to relocate. It didn't take a genius to understand that he'd executed this clever end run around Cartwright Energy and their fancy lawyers for her.

The big question was how?

She knew the value of the Connors' former parcel, and to her knowledge, he didn't have anywhere near that kind of money. At the last minute, she yanked the steering wheel to the right and skidded into the gravel drive that led to his house. She wasn't exactly anxious to see him again, but her father had taught her that some things were just better done in person.

Stepping out of her 4x4, she heard the whine of a circular saw coming from his living room. She went up on the porch and waited for a break in the noise before knocking. When he saw her, he looked almost as shocked to see her as she was to be there. But she'd made her choice, and now there was nothing to be done except see it through.

"Hey there, cowgirl." His nonchalant greeting sounded a bit strained, but he strolled over to look at her through the screen. "What brings you onto this side o' the fence?"

He looked tired, and there was a wariness

in those hazel eyes that made her feel sorry for him. He was expecting a dressing down, she realized, and in all honesty she couldn't blame him. Their last conversation hadn't ended well, and he had no reason to think this one would go any better. "I wanted to talk to you, if you have time."

His eyes narrowed suspiciously. "What'd I do now?"

"Something really sweet that I want to thank you for."

Understanding dawned, and he chuckled as he swung the door open. "Frank and Sally weren't supposed to tell you about all that."

"Why not? It was a wonderful thing to do. I don't know why you'd want to keep it a secret."

"Because it's me," he explained in a hesitant tone very unlike him, "and it's you."

"And that makes it complicated?" He nodded, and she sighed. "Yeah, I get that. We never seem to do anything the easy way, do we?"

That got her a look filled with a remorse so deep that she could almost feel it. "We used to. Then we grew up, and everything got tougher."

She couldn't have debated that if she wanted to, and she hunted for something to fill the silence stretching out between them. Glancing around the dusty room, her eyes landed on something in the middle of it all. Or rather, something that was no longer in the middle of it all.

Striding toward the fireplace, she stopped in front of it and picked up the only thing that was still displayed there: the framed print of Ty and her after competing at Cheyenne Frontier Days for the first time.

Photo in hand, she slowly turned to face him. "Tyler, where are your trophies?"

"Helena."

His jaw had tightened up the way it always did when he was hiding something, but this time she couldn't bring herself to get angry at him for keeping the truth from her. Walking toward him, she stopped when they were almost toe-to-toe. "What are they doing there?"

After a few moments, he rubbed his neck and gave her a sheepish look. "I sold them to a dealer so I could make the Connors a decent offer on that vacant land."

"Those were the last things you had from your rodeo career. Why on earth would you sell them?"

"I've still got Clyde," he corrected her, then tapped the frame with his finger. "And this. Besides, now there's a lot less to dust."

She laughed, and after a moment, he joined her. "You're not mad?"

"Mad?" she echoed in disbelief. "I'm grateful, and touched that you'd do something this generous for me. What I don't understand is that after the way we left things, why did you do it?"

"Isn't it obvious?" When she shook her head, he leaned in and kissed her cheek. Nosing along her jaw to her ear, he whispered, "I love you."

As he pulled back to give her one of those warm, lazy grins, she blinked up at him in astonishment. "You do?"

"For most of my life." Reeling her into his arms, he brushed a kiss over her lips that melted her heart on the spot. Resting his forehead against hers, he sighed. "Guess I just don't know how to stop."

And in that moment, she knew why she'd been so out of sorts lately. Why every time she thought of him, it took everything in her not to break down and cry. Reaching up, she bracketed his tanned face in her hands and gave him her very best smile. "Then I guess we're stuck with each other, because I don't know how to stop loving you, either."

Drawing him in for another kiss, she reveled in the feeling of being in his arms again, safe and protected by a man who'd given up his most valued possessions to secure the future of her mustangs. Not for his own gain, but because he knew how much that motley crew of ponies meant to her.

"Good to know," he said, a mischievous grin working its way across his features. "Y'know, I just had a thought."

"Will I like it?"

"Maybe. You know how you hate it when I call you MJ?"

She had no idea where this was going, but she laughed and played along. "Yes."

"How 'bout if I come up with something else?"

"That depends," she teased. "What did you have in mind?"

"Mrs. Tyler Wilkins." Lifting an eyebrow in a questioning look, he grinned. "Whattya think?"

Standing on tiptoe, she kissed him. "I think it's perfect."

Epilogue

Ties were really not his thing.

But you wore one to a wedding, Ty reminded himself as he pulled the twisted knot loose and began again. Especially when you were the groom.

A peek through the partially open door showed him that the small chapel was quickly filling with guests. He'd guess that more than a few were here to witness for themselves the minor miracle that was about to take place.

Him married to Morgan Whittaker. He still couldn't quite believe it himself. Recognizing that he hadn't gotten here on his own, he glanced up and murmured, "Thanks for the help."

His parents had flown in for the occasion, and each had come separately to see him to offer their congratulations and an envelope with a nice-sized check inside. It wasn't exactly warm and fuzzy family time, but he appreciated them making the effort all the same. Not to mention, the money would come in handy outfitting the room that Allie and Hannah had chosen to share when they moved into his bachelor pad. He was really glad he'd listened to Morgan's ideas for rehabbing the place. At least he didn't have to worry about her liking the decor in the home they'd all be living in.

Somehow, he and Morgan had gotten past their troubles and made their own family, he mused. A few months ago, he never could have pictured that, and now his long-held wish had become reality. Sometimes it was so unbelievable, he had to convince himself he wasn't dreaming.

A knock on the door brought him back to the present, and he opened it to find his younger brother on the other side. Ty pulled him into a hug and then set him away with a playful shove. "Robby! Man, am I glad to see you. Last time I looked out front, you weren't there. I was starting to think you got stuck in London on that business trip."

"I did, but I off-loaded some boring corporate junk and bolted. Sorry I'm late, but I had a stop to make on the way."

Without offering an explanation, he strolled back down the short hallway and disappeared around the corner. When he reappeared, he was pushing a wheelchair with their smiling grandfather as his passenger. Dressed in a crisp new suit, he waved at Ty. "There's my rodeo champ. Robby tells me there's a wedding today."

Of all the days for his grandfather to recognize him, none could have been more perfect. Ty swallowed around the lump that had formed in his throat and flashed his brother a grateful look. Kneeling beside the chair, he gave the frail man a gentle hug. "There is, and I'm so glad you could be here."

"I wouldn't miss your wedding. Are you marrying Morgan Whittaker?"

"Yes, sir, I am."

"Full of spit and vinegar, that one," Grandpa announced. "I always did like her."

"Yeah, me, too. Mom and Dad are here, if you wanna say hello to them."

The lined face wrinkled in distaste. "I think I'll sit with Robby. He doesn't give me a headache."

"I hear you." Standing, he gave his brother a grim look and murmured, "Dad wouldn't bring him. Said he didn't have time to drive over from the airport on his way here. I think it's interesting that you came across the Atlantic and managed to make it work."

"That's just him being lazy. Grandpa should be here, so I went to get him." Robby grimaced, disapproval plain in his eyes.

"It's a good thing we've got each other."

"Don't flatter yourself. When I get married, you'll owe me one."

Ty hadn't heard anything about a girlfriend being in the picture, so the offhand comment sparked his curiosity. "Should I be worried? Is another wedding coming up anytime soon?"

"Not if I have anything to say about it, so you're off the hook for a while."

Robby added a mischievous wink, which didn't do anything to settle the matter one way or the other. Fortunately, Grandpa's hearing was as sharp as it ever was

"Her name is Gretchen," he said, clearly pleased to be included in Robby's romantic secret. "She's from Switzerland, and she's very pretty."

"That's the last time I tell you anything," Robby grumbled, softening the threat with a good-natured look. "You liked her, didn't you?"

"You met her?" Ty asked.

"On Robby's fancy phone," he replied proudly. "We videoed her this morning."

"Video chatted," Romeo corrected him, chuckling at the misunderstanding. "She liked you, too."

"I don't doubt that for a second," Ty put in, shaking his head at their impromptu comedy routine. "You're the one in the family with all the charm."

"Guess we got it from you," Robby told him, patting his shoulder in a fond gesture that Ty completely understood.

Their strained relationship with their parents had left them with a special bond to each other and their easygoing grandfather. It had always seemed easier to talk to him, because he accepted what they did or said at face value, rather than scolding them simply for being boys.

All this reminiscing was tough on the nerves, Ty realized. It was a good thing he was only getting married once, because more than that would be more than he could take.

"So, we'll see you out there," Robby said, tipping the chair back in a wheelie to do a neat spin in the middle of the hallway.

"Don't drop the ring," Grandpa called over his shoulder.

"I won't," Ty assured him, laughing as he watched them go.

Once they were out of sight, he closed the

door and got back to what he'd been doing when they showed up. He'd restarted the tie for the fourth time when Perry came through the door holding a thin wrapped box in his hand. He took one look at Ty and laughed before handing it over. "Morgan sent you this."

Grateful for the distraction, he tore away the paper and opened the box. Inside the neatly folded tissue was a classy burgundy tie that would look great with the navy suit he'd worn during their trip to Washington. It was still the only one he had, so coordinating with it had been easy for her to do. As he lifted out her gift, he realized it was only half a tie. Laughing, he held up the clip-on accessory for Perry to see. "She knows me pretty well, doesn't she?"

"And she still wants to marry you. Go figure."

Ty knew he was kidding, but the comment mirrored what he'd been thinking. And when you added in the fact that he was about to officially become the daddy his daughters had been hoping for, he couldn't imagine himself ever having a more perfect day.

Finally satisfied with his reflection, Ty followed his best man out into the church to stand in the groom's customary waiting spot. The organist was playing some mellow hymns when Pastor Bartlett joined them. Giving Ty an encouraging smile, he said, "It's a beautiful day for a wedding."

"To be honest, I wouldn't care if it was a hundred degrees or a blizzard outside," Ty replied as Allie and Hannah appeared in the open doorway that led into the chapel. In their poufy white dresses and hair wreaths made of pink roses, they made him think of cherubs who had dropped in from heaven to make his life better. "The ladies coming in right now make every day good for me."

"That's really sweet," Perry murmured as the girls made their way up the aisle, sprinkling rose petals as they went. "Never knew you had it in you."

"I do now."

Smiling proudly at his daughters, he was surprised when they detoured from their practiced walk and bookended him in an enthusiastic hug. Taking their cue, he hunkered down and gathered them into his arms, looking from one to the other as his heart swelled with love for his little cowgirls.

Jessie came forward, flashing him a smile before herding the girls to the bride's side of the altar. She whispered something to them, then pointed back toward the door as the music ended and drifted into the rafters with dramatic effect. When that famous bridal march began, everyone stood, and Ty's gaze went to the doorway.

On her father's arm, Morgan was wearing the kind of smile he rarely saw. Light, unworried, full of joy, she made her way through the chapel as if she was floating on air. Her white dress swished over the runner, and the bouquet of pink roses she held matched the wreath nestled into a waterfall of luxurious blond curls. All at once, she was the tomboy he'd loved to chase and the woman he'd come to love more than anything in the world. Because of her, he was about to have the strong, loving family he'd always longed for. He couldn't envision his heart containing any more emotion than it did right now.

JD paused in front of him and gave him a stern look that he softened with a wink. Turning to Morgan, he broke etiquette and embraced his daughter tightly before letting her go. After shaking Ty's hand, he smiled at them both and rested his hands on their shoulders. "Be happy."

There were some "aws" in the crowd, and more than a few sniffles as JD took his seat next to Ryan and Ben. While folks were settling down, Ty took the opportunity to grin over at Morgan. "Nice dress."

"Nice tie," she shot back, adding a smirk for good measure.

He couldn't help laughing, and he heard his mother click her tongue from her seat in the front row. As usual, his behavior didn't suit her. Nothing new there, and he opted to ignore it. "You're gonna get me in trouble."

It was an old warning from when they were kids, and Morgan replied with what she'd always said back then. "You don't need my help."

They traded a smile and then got down to the business of getting married.

After a heartwarming homily about building a life together, the pastor gave folks time to get their cameras ready before turning to Ty. "Do you, Tyler Vernon Wilkins, take this woman, Morgan Jo Whittaker, to be your lawfully wedded wife?"

"I do." Taking her left hand, he slid the shining gold band into place.

"And do you, Morgan Jo Whittaker, take this man, Tyler Vernon Wilkins, to be your lawfully wedded husband?"

"I do."

He'd seen this woman stare down charging bulls, lasso calves and charm a contingent of politicians that would have made a lot of men turn tail and run. Somehow, this unflappable rancher's daughter fumbled his ring and it fell to the old wooden steps with a very audible thunk.

Jessie covered a laugh with her hand, and Perry was almost strangling behind him as Ty leaned down and retrieved it. Handing it back to his almost wife, he grinned. "Nervous, MJ?"

The sound of the nickname she hated had the effect he was after, as she squared her shoulders in a typical Morgan pose and successfully got the ring onto his finger.

"I now pronounce you man and wife. You may kiss the bride."

Before he could manage the last step in the ceremony, Allie and Hannah broke loose from their aunt and careened into them, nearly knocking them both over in their excitement.

"We're a family!" Hannah shouted joyfully, tossing her small bouquet into the air.

Allie followed along, and then shyly tugged on Ty's hand. When he looked down, she gazed up at him with a hopeful look. "Are you our daddy now?"

His already full heart swelled a little more, and he smiled over at the woman who'd been generous enough to give him the one more chance he'd needed. Pulling Morgan close, he kissed her and smiled.

"Yes, I am, honey. With Mommy's help, I finally got it right."

* * * * *

If you loved this tale of Western romance,
be sure to pick up
The Cowboy Takes a Wife
by Ruth Logan Herne.

And check out these other stories
from Mia Ross's previous miniseries,
Liberty Creek:

Mending The Widow's Heart
The Bachelor's Baby
His Two Little Blessings

Available now from Love Inspired!

Find more great reads at
www.LoveInspired.com

Dear Reader,

Welcome to Mustang Ridge!

I've always wanted to write a story set out West somewhere, and I had an absolute blast with this one. The idea came to me one night while my family and I were watching a documentary about a small town in Montana that was fighting against planned mining and energy development. What struck me was that the people waging this battle were everyday folks: farmers, ranchers and small business owners. They banded together to keep those changes from destroying the wild beauty of the land they treasured.

Morgan Whittaker stepped onto that same stage, strong, determined and ready to meet any challenge. Or so she thought. As capable as this rancher and single mom had always been, she quickly realized that her latest effort would require a team dedicated to keeping her hometown the way it was meant to be. She had plenty of courage when it came to animals and hard work, but taking on a challenge this huge required her to lean on her strong faith and trust in someone she'd long thought was out of her life forever.

After all he'd been through, Ty Wilkins

needed some of that faith himself to start his life over. He found it in the smiles of the daughters he met for the first time. Forging a connection with them instantly, he was willing to do whatever it took to be part of their lives. Forgiving himself for past mistakes was another story. Once he did, he was open to embracing a future with Morgan, creating the kind of family he'd always longed for.

This is just the beginning of the story of Mustang Ridge. I'm looking forward to finding out what happens next!

If you'd like to stop in and see what I've been up to, you'll find me online at www.miaross.com, Facebook, Twitter and Goodreads. While you're there, send me a message. I'd love to hear from you!

Mia Ross

Get 4 FREE REWARDS!

We'll send you 2 FREE Books plus 2 FREE Mystery Gifts.

Love Inspired® Suspense books feature Christian characters facing challenges to their faith... and lives.

FREE Value Over **$20**

2018 LOVE INSPIRED CHRISTMAS COLLECTION!

You'll get 1 FREE BOOK and 2 FREE GIFTS in your first shipment!

This collection is guaranteed to provide you with many hours of cozy reading pleasure with uplifting romances that celebrate the joy of love at Christmas.

YES! Please send me the first shipment of the 2018 Love Inspired Christmas Collection consisting of a FREE LARGER PRINT BOOK and 3 more books on free home preview. If I decide to keep the books, I'll pay just $20.25 U.S./$22.50 CAN. plus $1.99 shipping and handling. If I don't cancel, I will receive 3 more shipments, each about a month apart, consisting of 4 books, all for the same low subscribers-only discount price plus shipping and handling. Plus, I'll receive a FREE cozy pair of Holiday Socks (approx. retail value of $5.99)! As an added bonus, each shipment contains a FREE whimsical Holiday Candleholder (approx. retail value of $4.99)!

☐ 286 HCN 4330   ☐ 486 HCN 4330

Name (please print)

Address   Apt. #

City   State/Province   Zip/Postal Code

Mail to the Reader Service:
IN U.S.A.: P.O. Box 1867, Buffalo, NY. 14240-1867
IN CANADA: P.O. Box 609, Fort Erie, Ontario L2A 5X3